A History of the 21st Century

A Memoir by Major Alexander Pushkin Litvinova, U.S. Army, ret.

A Novella by Fred Beauford

A Neworld Review Book, an imprint of Morton Books, Inc

ISBN

978-1-929188-35-2

Other books by Fred Beauford

Fiction

The Womanizer

The Year Jerry Garcia Died

Orphans

The King of Macy's

The African Gentleman and the Plot to Re-establish the New World Order

The Hard Luck Novel

Non-Fiction

The Rejected American

The First Decade: Essays, 2002-2010

Fred Beauford: Reviews

,,,and Mistakes Made Along the Way (Memoir)

Collaboration

Meditations and Ascension: Black Writers on Writing with Dr. Brenda M. Greene

Resistance and Transformation, with Dr. Brenda M, Greene

The University Press of Mississippi Literary Conversation Series

Conversations with Ernest J. Gaines

Conversation with Albert Murray

Conversations with John A. Williams

Prologue

Dec. 12, 2093

Dear Father:

I have wanted to write to you for years. I kept putting it off, pushing away the pen, the precious, hard to find paper, promising myself that I would soon sit down and do so, telling myself over and over again that I was really not the great writer as you, telling myself over and over again that I was wasting a key resource thinking I had something important to say.

However, just yesterday, the day after my 90th birthday, the day before the 80th year since your death, it was on that day that the light came, and I knew it was time to write you.

You have cast a long shadow over my life, Father; yet I never felt that I fully understood you, or your century, or your grand obsessions, or even your deep love for my mother.

How could it have happened? She, a poor immigrant from the grand heart of Russia, a former Communist.

"Ah, yes!" Mother said to me shortly before she died, now not the beautiful, 39 year old woman you fell in love with, but a tiny, wizen, frail, drawn old lady, with less then a year to live, and only three years before the Big Bang.

"Ah, yes!" she croaked again, now with a slight, subtle touch of theatrical flair. It was on that last 'ah, yes' that I knew she was still an actress, as old as she was. She wasn't fooling me.

Her worn, cracked face suddenly came alive, and filled with delight at the old, pleasant memory. Her Russian accent, through now shaky, was still as heavy as always. "He asked 'what was it like to be a Communist?"

"Yes, mother," I replied as gently as possible, glad to see her smiling again, and not wanting to tire her by her telling me this story yet again.

"I remember reading one of his stories," I said to her in Russian, the words I had read years ago coming back to me. "I knew it was you and him he was writing about. You just shook your lovely blond head and laughed a small laugh, revealing even, child-like teeth, and you said to him, 'oh, Communist'.

"You laughed once again, eyeing him nervously, as if seeing him for the very first time, although you two worked closely together in a large department store selling ties. Yes, mother, I remember reading that."

***

Dear Father, it is only through your writing that I really know you. You were an old dude when I was born. I know you tried your best, but you know that you were too old to take me to the park to play tennis, as all the other kids did with their father's on the weekends.

And mother, she was also older than most moms, not as old as you were, obviously. But she looked after me, worked, and did her art, and worked some more. As you once wondered in one of your stories, did she really come all the way from Mother Russia for this?

Mother was your long sought-after Muse, however. Your brilliant, insightful writings after you met her testify to that. Even as I have gained the courage to write, I still do not fully understand the Muse.

What does it do to you, father? What was it that you found so wonderful, so magical in Mother that released so many wise words into the future, because all of those ideas are still very much a part of us today, at the dawn of yet another century. Maybe more so.

As my century nears its chaotic end, for many reasons I can't even begin to articulate, I now desperately want to understand yours, which is why I'm writing you.

Father, in many ways, your century was our great cross to bear. So much was released on the world. Capital ran wild. Greed had become the norm, and America made a bizarre transformation at the beginning of my century into a self-righteous, militaristic bully.

There have been all kinds of reasons given. Even today, if you can believe that, people are still trying to figure it out. You know what I think. I think it was television. I think it just made people stupid. But what do I know, Father. I wasn't there. Still, most said it was because of September 11, which unknown at the time, foreshadowed much of what was to come.

I was not born yet when that horrible thing happened. But I know from watching history on television that September 11 only slowed down America, and if anything, made the international money class even stronger. Nothing could stop their onward march to completely dominate the planet.

The world had never seen anything quite like this, and for years was cowed and stunned into a passive silence and inaction, until finally, someone acted. But we will get to that later.

Mother loved Pushkin. But when you wanted to name me Alexander Pushkin Mother told me how hard she protested.

"No, no, no, no, no," she said to you

"Why not," you answered. "Pushkin was the great African-Russian, like my son will be, and Alexander was the great conqueror, like he will also be."

"But that's not Russian. It's vulgar to combine names like that."

"Well this ain't Russia, dear."

Mother said she just threw up her hands, and that's why she named me Alexander Pushkin Litvinova, giving me her last name.

In the end, she didn't care about proper Russian. She loved you so much. Maybe it was just your blackness she couldn't help loving after spending so many cold, long lonely nights in her crowded flat in Moscow, dreaming of a dark, handsome Pushkin? And you were dark, indeed, not one of those washed out types

Now, she had found her own poetic Pushkin in, of all places, the unpoetic, material world of late 20th Century America.

But how romantic we Russians! Everyone else comes to America seeking to find a Millionaire. But Mother came to America and found a poet, a black poet, just like Pushkin. No wonder we Russians are open to big ideas like Communism; or are easily seduced by large notions of art, poetry and romantic love, unlike practical, material Americans.

I once asked Mother, "Isn't it funny that we Russians were once raised on no God, but we still clung to beliefs in art and romantic love, even in the worse days of Communism and depredation of our faith; and blessed, rich Americans embraced God, but seems to believe in nothing that cannot be touched, or consumed."

Mother just laughed. "You just like your father, Alex," she said to me. She pointed at her head. "Always thinking. But you're wrong. That's American thinking."

"What do you mean, Mother? What's American thinking?"

"Russians are religious. We stayed religious. You can't believe in love and art and not be religious." She started nervously rubbing the little gold cross she always wore, eyeing me carefully.

I stood corrected. I understood her insight. She was really agreeing with me. I knew Communism couldn't change a people's basic nature, as Lenin foolishly believed. I just wasn't as good at expressing ideas as you were.

There was also another major difference between me and you Father. Before the Big Change, I was a 21st Century man of action, not thought. Mother was only trying to make me feel good by saying I was just like you, always thinking. I was always thinking alright, but not about the kinds of things you thought about. There was action, and huge amounts of money to be had, and babes, nightlife.

All that race stuff that so concerned you didn't mean that much anymore, as long as you got with the program

It is clear now, that your generation was the last one that dared to really think. I mean really think. Before the Big Change, after I left college, I would only occasionally pick up one of your books, or any book for that matter, and then only to please Mother. I wasn't alone. None of us read even the few newspapers that were left, and all that pointless noise online, which was solely in the hands of the elites—was something to avoid like the plague.

Besides, other than movie crap, so much of the stuff the few people who did still read and write was about the so-called "lessons" of Sept. 11 and the long wars that followed. Who needed that shit!

Now at 90, I have finally gotten the courage, and have broken the curse of my generation, and all the generations that came after us. And you know what, Father, it feels damn good so far!

I think I have become the great Alexander Pushkin, just as you and Mother wanted me to become when you named me. Finally! At last!

How clever, how literary, how terrible artful, Father: You, a so-called African-American; your lovely Muse, a Russian, a former Communist, an actress, a belly dancer, a romantic, a dreamer of big dreams—to name me Alexander Pushkin.

Now I see why, Father! Now I am ready at last to live up to my name. I feel the pulse of the New World in every vein of my body, as much as the part black Pushkin felt the very pulse of Russia, as he defined the Russian soul.

I am ready, Father.

CHAPTER 1

It was 11:43, October 3, 2037. That day proved to be the major turning point for my century, our defining moment, so to speak. I remember that day also because it was so glorious.

I had walked the beach for hours, the first time I had done so in months. Those days, just as now, it was impossible to predict the weather. It could be hot. It could be cold. It could snow in June, or be 100 in October! There was chaos all over the globe.

In America, a seemly permanent shift in the jet stream had parked a cloud over all of the West Coast, and Southern California, where you and Mother first met, and where I was born, was now one of the coolest, wettest places on earth. The Southeast, on the other hand, was slowly turning into a desert. The ice caps had increased, which dismayed many, and there were now big, unmending, scary holes all over the ozone.

Everyone knew why. We had long known what we were doing to the earth. Even you, my own father, was one of those "warners" I was so disdainful of. I read your books of essays; I knew what you were warning us about.

But America had beaten the Russians, and brought you and mother together; and beat the living shit out of the Radical Muslins—those sneaky bastards. We were the mightiest power ever, and this had brought us prosperity. Who the hell needed warners, Father?

***

I first saw the bright light, Father, followed by an awesome explosion. Then my DYE suddenly went dead. I didn't panic. I knew instantly what had happened. But why here? Why now? Was it isolated? Was the sky all at once going to be filled with bright lights and awesome explosions?

I ran to the DYE hanging on my white walls and tried everything, but nothing. I suddenly felt a wave of warm energy sweep over me. Not a heavy wave, but a small, gentle, caressing, barely noticeable one.

The blast that caused it was either very small, or so far away that it had little affect on where I was living in Brighton Beach.

***

That surprise you, don't it, Father?

No, not the blast. That shouldn't have surprised you. You knew that was coming.

No, the fact that I was living in Brighton Beach, a young man in the last years of his thirties, still unmarried, still without children. This was Mother's apartment. But she had died three years before the Big Bang, so it was my apartment.

***

Excuse me for a few moments, Father. Your youngest grandson, Nicholas, just let himself in. He will be 22 in a few weeks, a born Scorpio. You should see him! What a fine specimen of a human being! He is 6'4 and has a charismatic, towering presence, and an adorable baby face. I just love him!

I didn't do to bad for an old man, did I! All is not bad in this Century. If you got the right stuff, you can live forever, especially now that we have gotten rid of most of that electronic bullshit that had poisoned us, poisoned the earth and imprisoned our minds.

It seems that you left me the greatest gift of all: precious melanin. Melanin is now worth all the gold in the world, and is earth's only real hope for a human presence.

Imagine that, Father. Imagine that! And our handsome Nicky is full of melanin.

"Hi dad, how are you feeling? You ok?" he asked the last time he visited, with almost youthful indifference.

"Oh, I'm alright, Nicky," I answered. I shyly looked away from him and sighed slightly, with a taste of fake melancholy I had learned from Mother; as if to say if he really cared, he would look in on me more often.

Now that he is old enough, he lives in a group home with his three official wives. He can only drop in on me two or three times a month, if I'm lucky.

"Are you sure dad?" I could see real concern on his handsome young face. He had my color; in fact, he was a little darker, and he is large, and well built like I once was, but he looked a lot more like his mother.

She was also Russian, just like my mother. She died of skin cancer just two years ago at only 58. She was as blond and beautiful as your Sasha was.

But Lucy, as darling as she was, just did not have the same magic as my mother, the magic of the Muse. In fact, she had few muse-like qualities. All she had was raw nerves of steel. She was one badass bitch!

Your two other grandsons now live in Florida, the great desert. Unfortunately, my two boys are both fair skinned and I have long warned them to beware the sun, and stay as far north as they could.

Why take chances? Everyone with white skin, and any sense, never ventured further south than South Carolina, and have especially fled places like Florida; but some, like my two boys, take it almost as a dare.

"Melanin, dad," Varsia, the oldest, the one with the blond hair, said to me just before they left. "That sun can't get us."

I only laughed at his foolishness. But what could I say? In many ways, I had failed them. I was not able to impart to them fully the great gift I was able to give to Nicky. They had to go, however. I knew that. But I also knew, despite my brave front, that I didn't want my two boys out there facing that dreadful, deadly sun.

I mean, it was bad enough here in Brooklyn, Father! But I also knew that there was land, and a black bride, the grandest prize of all, if you could just deal with the sun.

Brave, 20-year-old Varsia, and his younger brother Nikita, were already dressed in the long, white, loose flowing robes with hoods, that many whites around the world had adopted before they ventured outdoors.

Nikita, who had inherited my bold flamboyance, his Grandmother's theatrical flair, and perhaps your intellectual daring, dramatically pulled out a pair of dark, wide sunglasses, and put them on, and poked out his full lips at his brothers and me.

"Am I wracked, Mr. Major, or what!"

I laughed again. "Nikita, don't fuck with me boy! You're wracked alright. If I were still in the Army, I would have your dumb ass arrested, and thrown under the jail! You guys look ridiculous! You look like damn Aussies. I'm damn glad Nicky ain't old enough to be running after you two fools!" I said, laughing again at my two young boy's getup.

Still, my laughter was tinged with much pride. I loved their youthful bravado. Thirteen-year-old Nicky just looked on enviously. As I glanced over at him, I could see that he would have liked for nothing better than to join his two foolish older bothers.

I didn't know if they had enough melanin to protect them. But they were adventurous young men, seeking their black brides, so they had to go where there was still hope of finding one.

Still, they are so fair that some folks used to ask if I had adopted them; that they were just two more white orphans.

"Listen my young Nicky," I said in a fit of old man grouchiness, "who do you think I am? One of those weak-ass white sissies who drop at the age of 50! I'm an African! We live forever!"

I gave my son the best-wrinkled wink I could muster. His innocent, young face lit up with delight, and he started laughing loudly and I saw once again his mother, and my mother.

"Yeah, dad. You are some African! All these years I thought you were Russian!"

"Now, now Nicky," I said, feeling a little disappointed in him.

"Ok, dad, you're African," he said, giving in slowly. "But dad, I want you to resign from that damn re-education committee. I know you're still a big hero, after you and mother saved the world, but you're too old to be running to meetings and listening to all that bullshit! If folks ain't re-educated by now, when will they be?"

Oh, here we go with that again! I especially loved the remark about how Lucy and I saved the world! We kicked some serious ass alright, but it wasn't just us. But I wasn't up for a fight with my favorite person in the world.

"We'll see," I said, mainly because I wanted to see his handsome face happy, the face that so much reminded me of my precious Lucy. And although he might not see it as clearly as I, I also see the mighty African written all over his face.

"Listen to me, dad," he said impatiently. With that, he headed straight to the kitchen, his favorite place to be.

"I cooked some collard greens, Nicky. We have to return to our African roots you know! By the way, I heard from Nikita and Varsia!" I yelled after him.

***

Dear, Father, I'm back. I know that young innocent Nicky thinks I'm a little crazy. The way this letter to you is going, you probable think the same thing. Now that I have started writing, I now clearly remember an essay you wrote about how blacks were non-linear thinkers. As writers, we Russians are more famous for the long, linear narrative, just the opposite of you blacks.

By the way, I guess you noticed by now that I say we when I speak of Russians, or Russia. It is because mother raised me that way, and because

I have always felt the tug of Mother's homeland calling to me, more than I ever felt the pull of this place we call America.

Although I have never stepped foot on its sacred soil, I know we have a rich culture in Mother Russia, heavily influenced by my namesake. It is a culture based on more than money and material things.

I also knew in the deepest recesses of my mind that I was playing a game; that I was trying to have it both ways, Father. As much as I said I hated the based, consumer culture that had once again come to dominate America after the fear of terror following Sept. 11, and the years of endless war—with me delighting my friends in our fancy clubs in Manhattan with my clever put downs, and calling myself a black Russians, much to loud laughter.

"We Russians have something you dodo birds don't have—it's called culture, duh! You basketball playing, movie watching mothers."

"Oh, please, P, give it up!" my friend David would soon say, laughing, and waving away my nonsense with a decided wave of his hand, and everyone would join in.

My friends knew, and I knew, that in the end, I was one with them, even as I called myself a Russian. I thoughtlessly consumed as much as everyone else, and was more than ready to go to war to protect my right to consume even more, just like everyone else.

It was just that I was the one with the communist Russian mother, Father: an actress, a dancer, a romantic; and the brilliant, thoughtful, concerned African-American writer, who was my father, but who also left behind all of those questions for future generations to ponder--questions that went to the very heart of who I had really become.

So, now as I try to write, I hope you can see just how wired my internal self is to both the Russian and the African-American. So, you know that this letter to you will jump all over the place, because not only am I black, but an *old* black.

Chapter Two

Ok, where was I? Bare with me, Father. Ok, I was talking about the bomb. Or Mother? Or Nicky? Or was it Brighton Beach? No, it was the bomb! The Bomb. The famous Bomb!

That beautiful day in October, everyone's favorite nightmare came true. someone detonated a portable nuclear bomb right in the center of Manhattan. Movies, television dramas and novels have long tried to portray such an event, almost as if everyone knew it was inevitable. But this was no movie, or novel. This was cold-blooded reality.

I could have been there, Father, with me now nothing but a whiff of ash.

My office was near ground zero. But this was a rare, beautiful fall day, and I was thinking about Mother. For some reason, a strong, overwhelming urge to talk to her came over me, an aching almost.

I walked the near empty Brighton Beach all morning, thinking of her, thinking of the California I remembered before the rains came, thinking that a blue ocean was better than a gray one, thinking about how much I had meant to her. I would occasionally nod to a passerby as I walked all the way to Coney Island, and stared once again at the rusted parachute drop, left by a world long, long gone.

I slowly headed back to Brighton Beach. I couldn't bring myself to get on the D train, or one of the express buses, and make the long ride to my office in Manhattan. I didn't feel like selling dumb movies, or selling dumb anything for that matter. I felt Mother talking to me.

She was right, whatever she said to that day. She saved my life, Father. She kept me on that near empty beach, just she and I, and her wise conversation. She knew what was going to happen, and reached out and saved me!

At this time, Manhattan was at its peak, the very zenith of its worldwide control. Even powerful Hollywood had packed up and left a cold, wet, dreary California and settled fully in Manhattan and Queens. Hollywood was the last jewel in our crown. Old 20th Century despots like Franco, Idi Amin, Chairman Mao, Peron, Hitler, or mother's Stalin, could only have shook their evil old heads, and marveled in dumb-struck awe.

It wasn't the old, two-fisted Capitalist that Karl Mark feared and hated so much. Of course there were still those headline-grabbing billionaires running all over the place. But they were in the end, merely a sideshow, someone to help sell newspapers and magazines, and entertain us on the DYE, with tall tales of their many dalliances.

Rather, it was money, and cold, faceless, dedicated, efficient Managers that had done what force of arms, or big ideas could not do: conquer the world!

Although no one would point to the obvious, in many ways, Karl Mark had won.

But as always Father, there is a price to be paid for everything.

After the Big Bang, as if was henceforth known, with capitalized letters and all, the highly formidable American military machine once again went on full alert. I was a proud Major in the Army Reserves. I was co-commander of a Tank battalion, and I immediately reported for duty, ready to kick some serious ass.

But who committed the deed? We had subdued the Muslim world. So it couldn't be them. Weren't they now our friends? Wasn't there now hundreds of Macdonald's in every Muslim state on the planet? Didn't over 15 million Muslims live peacefully within our boarders?

What unnerved us so much, besides the dirty deed itself, was the outburst of spontaneous celebrations all over the globe.

For example, hordes of happy, dancing people poured into the nighttime streets of Paris, as over a million people laughed, sang, danced and smashed every Pizza Hut they could find, in a joyful, tearful celebration. It was if a heavy gray blanket had been lifted off of the world.

But what were they celebrating? The day of the event, I was suddenly startled as my DYE came back on. Power was back. I switch to television and the full horror, which I knew instinctively, had happened, unfolded.

How could anyone want to celebrate that, Father?

The cute commercials were gone, perhaps forever. Now it was just days, and weeks, and months of death, and more death. The damage from the bomb was worse than horrendous. I can't even begin to describe the horror, made even more horrible because all of my friends, and my girlfriend and best friend were murdered that day, with not even a trace left of their existence: the same bright, young, gifted friends that would occasionally come slumming out to Brighton Beach to visit the "mad Russian."

Gina, my golden, brown-skinned, 27 year-old Filipino girlfriend, was short, with wide hips and a broad nose and small button lips, which she supplied with endless amounts of bright, perfumed red lipstick. She also had large, white gleaning teeth, and her breath often smelled of garlic. She was so smart. So to the point. So full of life. So sexual. So much energy.

My oldest friend, the pale, nervous, overweight, thoughtful David, the brilliant gay book editor of *The New Yorker,* had told me just last week that he was sick of what he was doing, this endless chattering about so-called stars and wayward billionaires.

"I hate my job. We're fiddling, and Rome is about to burn to the fucking ground, P! All we do is watch movies that tell us nothing. Television sucks. Our books stink. Our brains have died. Can't you see what's happening, P? There is something sick about all of this. Something is very wrong, man," he said.

I felt for my friend. He was asking questions that I, and most of us, had long learned not to ask. Just go along with the program.

"Lighten up David! You got the best job in New York. What else would you do?"

David phased slightly. A genuinely puzzled look appeared on his pale face. I have never seen someone so white and pasty-faced all the time, even in summer. "Who knows, go write a book, or something," he answered finally.

We both laughed at that one! Only entertainers wrote books that anyone bothered to read. Everyone knew that. Book editor. He was right, although I didn't say so to his face. His job was a joke.

How poor David must have instantly known just how right he really was, as all of him just vanished, evaporated, and melted into nothingness.

And Peter, Rebecca, and my best bar friend, the handsome, black Malik. They all laughed at me because I lived in Brighton Beach, in Mother's old apartment, and not in the rich, famous, fabulous Manhattan.

But so what! Brighton Beach was cozy, old world, and on October 12, 2037, still very Russian. All over New York City, money had pushed working people out to the hated suburbs. And this was the very edge of Brooklyn, far away from the greedy grasp of Manhattan. So, many old Russians still hung on. That's why Mother brought me here from California. That's why she loved it. And that's why I loved it. And now it had saved my life.

The bomb had been planted in the subway right at 34th Street. This had the added affect of the shock waves traveling aggressively through the many underground tunnels. Most of Manhattan just imploded onto itself.

Even today, years later, no one knows how many people were killed. Manhattan as always, was loaded to the gills with Masters and Mistress of the Universe, and the best and brightest, which were my gifted friends.

Someone once estimated that there were only 300,000 of us in all of New York City, out of a total population of 10 million. But we 300,000 were the brains. We wrote the scripts. We provided the narrative. We provided the dash, the fun. We made the whole damn thing worthwhile. And we ran the whole damn world.

And now, with the exception of me, lonely me, they were all dead!

How many? Two million? Three million? We will never know. What we did know was this was the largest death toll in a single event triggered by human anger, in the history of the planet. And we know that America creased being what it had become.

Soon, our first "Hispanic" President, George P. Bush, 3rd, was on the air gravely telling us that whoever did this would not escape the might of America.

President Bush was also one lucky man. Maybe the voice of his mother, or his grandmother, Barbara, whispered something to him that day, just as Mother had whispered something to me, because he was suppose to have been in New York to address an urgent UN conference on our worsening weather, which he maintained was just alarmist bullshit!

He suddenly came down with a case of the California Flu, a new strain that was killing scores of people in many parts of the country, but especially in California. Bush didn't die from the flu, however. And he didn't die from the bomb that many say was really meant for him.

Wags even started calling the attack "The Bush Curse" in that every time a Bush got into office, all hell broke loose.

In immediate response to the attack, President Bush sent out to all the oceans of the world our mighty warships; he ordered our brave, well-trained troops, including my outfit, equipped with the best weapons on planet Earth, onto ships and planes.

***

This is an aside, Father, but I especially loved our new tank. I know that you didn't serve in the military; that you were an artist and intellectual. But goddamn it, Father, my new tank was made of lightweight plastic. Yes, plastic, Father! Can you believe that? It was a major breakthrough. No more of those heavy-assed tanks. This new beast was not only light, but was as fast as life itself; fast and extremely deadly, with a main gun so accurate that it could blow the shit off the ass of a mosquito at 300 yards!

And shells just bounced off of it.

I know that you can tell from the way my writing has suddenly picked up, so to speak, that this is turning me on. Forgive an old man's highly selective memory, Father, but I loved the tank corp. They wanted to eliminate tanks; said they were useless. That was bullshit! We wouldn't let them take our tanks away!

I also loved the uniforms. I loved the grand parades, with brave, purposeful men and women of action, saluting and strutting and swaggering, and pulling rank on each other.

I remember one parade in particular, Father, at Fort Hood, Texas. Our outfit had just ended two months in the field on full division maneuvers.

"Grand day for a parade, Major!" the Old Man said to me. He was looking as spry as always.

"Grand day, Indeed, sir," I answered.

My friend Colonel Bird had joined me on the reviewing stand we shared with a two star, a Brigadier, four full birds and an assortment of Light Colonels and Majors.

We all smartly exchanged salutes and then looked on proudly as the good old red, white and blue of the greatest flag on earth, ever; the colorful battalion flags; the red flags of the artillery; the blue flags of the mighty infantry; and of course, the bright yellow flags of the legendary, ass-kicking Cavalry—flew proudly by, with bands loudly playing strutting, ass-kicking music.

DUNNA, DUN, DUNNA DUN DA DUN, DUNNA DUN TA DUN, DUNNA DUN DUN DA DUN!

Talk about Pomp and Circumstance! This was great stuff, Father.

All of this was right up my alley. I told you that I was a man of action, not thought. I told you at the very beginning of this letter that I was no damn intellectual!

I loved moving briskly down an open field in full formation, all our tanks lined up, charging forward, our big guns booming all over the place, machine guns blazing, TATTATTATTATTAT, planes and helicopters flying all around, bombs going off, smoke and fire everywhere; and me whooping and hollowing like a madman, yelling orders to my troops and driver to "kick it in the ass!"

Occasionally, I would lapse into Russian, but my troops knew what I meant.

I only once had someone shooting back at me with live ammo, ready to blow my crazy black Russian ass to Kingdom come! That's when we had to go back to the Mid-east in 29 and kick some uppity butt. You would have thought those dumbbells would have learned not to mess with us again. But that's when I won most of my medals, and picked up some lead in the right shoulder for my effort.

But enough war stories, Father. You know how we old guys are. We just love sitting around telling war stories. I'm already wiping away tears just thinking about the good times I had.

God, Father, I loved that shit!

***

Now I was floating around the ocean with my state-of-the-art tank, and equally deadly airplanes and missiles were ready and fully armed, just waiting for President's Bush's orders. We had enough firepower to blow up every square inch of the planet earth.

But who were we to attack? President Bush didn't seem to know. The Joint Chiefs didn't know. No one knew.

Should we attack the French, because they laughed at our culture, and hated out hamburgers, and were still pissed off because we thwarted their plans to build a counterweight to our power? The black Africans, because we stood by as they killed each other in unbelievable numbers, and because we did little to help them fight AIDS, and now they have a population on the entire continent of only 200 million. The Muslims who still curse us silently under their beards? The Russians? The South American? The world, because our greed poisoned the world?

We had watched in horror as instantly, everywhere people started celebrating. But the governments of the earth all expressed deep sympathy for us, and firmly denounced their misguided citizens who danced in the streets.

There were also no Bin Ladens to point the finger at. And no Bin Ladens came forward nowhere on earth. Not from the Mid-east. Not from Africa. Not from France. Not from South America.

All over the world, everyone was begging for our mercy, saying: "we didn't do it! We didn't do it!"

Soon, the order came for us to stand down. I was very angry and disappointed, Father, as I addressed my troops. As our CO, Lieutenant Colonel Jack "Blackjack" Bird sternly looked on, I told them, with my voice shaking with anger and bitterness, that what happened to New York, that what happened to my friends, that what happened to this great country, would not go un-revenged.

"Some of you men and women will return to normal life, until called again, if we can ever have normal life again in America. I say yes we can members of the 36th Calvary. Let's not let those cowards who killed so many of us win. We even lost members of our own outfit. But we are still strong, my friends. Still strong. Let's not let them destroy the American Dream. So go back my friends, and keep building, and keep the promise of America alive."

So for now, our ships were called back, our planes grounded, and I was able to take off my uniform, although this was now the only job I had.

Chapter 3

Dear Father, this is getting a little too heavy and sad for me. Let's take a break for a while from October 3, 2037 and let me tell you a little more about the life Mother and I lived after you died. But you can see how the Big Bang was the turning point for human life on this planet!

Your Sept. 11, although horrible to be sure, was still, compared to what I lived through, small potatoes.

You died in 2010, twenty-eight years before the Big Bang. Mother moved us to Brighton Beach a year later, following a horrific incident. She always told me that the reason why the two of you were never married in a formal sense, was because of her husband, the one she came over with from Russia.

He would not give her a divorce. He was obsessed with her. You Father, must have had some nerve, or you must have wanted her badly, to move in with her with such a crazy man lurking in the shadows.

Just after you died, one night as she returned for a rehearsal, she spotted him out of the corner of her eye. The cold rains had just started pounding California. This night, the rain poured down on Mother as she ran from her car to the door of our apartment house. For some reason, she parked on the street and not inside, which was her big mistake.

After all these years, she had thought that it was over. But there he was, his body drenched, his eyes hollowed, his clothes disheveled, a broken, crazed look on his gaunt face. A latter day Rasputin.

She dropped her keys. "Leave me alone!" she shouted.

He continued toward her, and grabbed her by the arm.

"You dirty bitch!" he said harshly in Russian, in a voice filled with hated.

Mother broke away from him and started to run. She ran out into the wet street in oncoming traffic in hopes that someone would stop and help her.

Her mad husband caught her from behind and spun her around. He yelled another curse in Russian and smashed her squarely in the mouth with his fist. She felled backwards awkwardly.

Before he could do any more damage to her, a female motorist stopped her car and started yelling and blowing her horn loudly.

Mother's husband ran off. By now, more cars had stopped, and in the distance, a police siren could already be heard approaching.

The courageous woman who had perhaps saved Mother's life, came over and cradled her head, unmindful of the cold, pouring rain, and the fact that Mother's blood was pouring out of her mouth onto the woman's garments.

"Now, now," she said softly, gently rocking Mother back and forth. "It'll be alright. He's gone. It'll be alright."

Mother spat three of her front teeth out onto the woman, and started crying heavily, in loud, heart-broken sobs, just like a young child.

I remember when the police brought her home. I can still hear the loud sounds of their radios, as those radios sputtered and crackled with the shorthand of the official business of police work.

Mother had refused to go to the hospital because she knew I was home alone, waiting for her.

"Mother!" I screamed. "Who did this to you?" And I knew the answer before she even answered.

She was a mess. She was shaking and shriveling with cold and fright. Her entire body was soaking wet; her hair was laying flat on her head; her beautiful face and her clothes were covered with blood.

She kept her hands to her mouth to hide the missing teeth from me. The same even, child-like teeth you so admired in your stories, were now gone.

"It was that fuckin' bastard prick Sergie, Wasn't it!" Tears were running down my face and I was cursing in Russian for the first time ever in front of Mother.

I pushed myself passed the two policewomen, and threw my arms around her, and bitter, hateful, helpless tears poured from me as my small body shook with anger.

Mother started gently rubbing my head to comfort me.

"Now, now, Alex," she said, holding me tightly. "Now, now."

But I hated Sergie! I hated that bastard.

Sergie didn't know it, and neither did Mother, but although I was only eleven, I knew some mean Cholos! I didn't go to school with any because Mother sent me to private school, but I knew some. I saw them in the park with their shaved heads and tattoos.

I was now going to become a Cholo, and we were going to get Sergie for beating up my mother, if it was the last thing I did!

***

I didn't become a Cholo, Father. I never got the chance. Mother's husband was soon arrested. Because of the sheer violence of the attack, and the fact that the courts had warned him to stay away from her many, many times, he was finally deported back to Russia.

But Father, Mother was never the same again after that dreadful night. For her, living in Southern California, the golden land, the land of big dreams, was instead a big nightmare. Not only had the once wonderful sun started to disappear, but also everywhere there was pain. Pain from her memories and lost of you. Pain from a crazy, disappointed husband. Pain from broken, unrealized dreams.

She had a cousin who had moved to Brighton Beach at the same time she and Sergie had moved to Los Angeles, which was right after Communism ended, and the gates were let opened. So the move was made to Brooklyn.

***

Before you start feeling too much pain for Mother, New York turned out to be just the right thing for both of us. Life improved dramatically. I loved New York the moment I looked out the plane window and saw all of those big buildings. I was twelve, and guess what, I had never walked in snow! Growing up, I saw some on the mountains near us in the Valley, which in the last few years seemed to always be covered with snow. But I never walked and played in it.

Mother used to say that what she missed most about Moscow was the soft, cold, white snow.

The two of us arrived in the middle of January, when winter was still winter. New York was covered with a white, heavy recent "Storm of The Century"!" It was beautiful, Father.

For the first time in my young life I ran through snow with all the unbridled joy of youth, laughing and jumping up and down, and happily throwing snowballs at Mother.

And Mother, she was all smiles now, as if she was back in her beloved Moscow.

We settled into the one bedroom apartment in Brighton Beach that was to be my home for many, many years.

Chapter 4

All right Father, I can hear you thinking impatiently, "for God's sake, enough with the snow! Get on with it boy! What happened after the so-called Big Bang?" Ok, Father. Just remember, however, I'm not the great storyteller as you.

Sure, I used to hold my friends spell-bounded with my stories, something I must have gotten from you and Mother, but that was the spoken word. This writing stuff is something different.

But let us forge ahead anyway. As to be expected, Father, things started getting really weird in America after that. The Bomb was not only an enormous, destructive explosion, but it was also a particularly "dirty bomb," as the scientists later explained to us.

That means that Manhattan is still off-limits, even some 54 years later. Could it have been 54 years, Father? Wow, that's longer than most white people live these days! I've been hanging on longer than I ever knew, especially since everyone around me are dropping like flies.

Meanwhile, stupid, damn, dumb-ass fools are always being arrested for trying to sneak into Manhattan, looking for all those diamonds and other valuables buried underneath all of that red hot rubble!

In a few years, President Bush was voted out of office. We didn't know it at the time, but this was going to be the next to last time we voted directly for our leaders.

By the way, Father, we found out who set off the bomb. You probably guessed it anyway. It was homegrown, not some mad terrorist from abroad. The last straw for the small group that carried out the nefarious deed, was the release of two news items that became the big deal of the day.

The first, which garnered little attention at first, but slowly became a major scandal, and did more to undermine America's great confidence than any Big Idea from Russia or those crazy-ass dudes from the Mid-east—was so horrendous in its implication, that even someone as apolitical as I, wanted to hang someone.

It seemed that as far back as the last century, the automobile and oil industries knew that at the present level of consumption, the world as we knew it would become unfit for human life. They knew it! Their own scientists said so! Our government also knew about the secret documents that outlined the deadly results.

They also knew how to build vehicles that wouldn't kill the earth, but worked in concert to suppress any such invention from coming on-line.

They were willing to kill their own grandchildren to live in the moment of great wealth, to show off in the pages of Forbes! What madness, Father.

The other bit of news that caused a sensation was the definitive proof that Mars once had thriving life forms, and what we know as civilization.

But something happened to their world, and they lost their climate, and everything turned to rust, and gradually disappeared, leaving just a bare trace of what had been. It was only when we sat foot on the planet and started to explore did we uncover the clues.

Now most scientist believe that it was Mars that first breathed life into earth; that we were contaminated, if you will, either by conscious probes, or by just pieces of Mars breaking off and landing in our oceans.

In essence, we are Martians!

Now, I guess that got your attention, Father! I told you that my century was interesting. The idea that we are really Martians is an old idea that sic-fi writers have been playing with for centuries. But now we had proof.

Well, anyway, Father, the group that blew up Manhattan put two and two together as far as they were concerned. The Martian's probably destroyed themselves by not taking care of their environment, they reasoned in the Manifesto they finally issued.

The same Manifesto, we learned later, that caused President Bush to order us to stand down, and quit wasting precious resources searching for phantom enemies.

Our backyard enemies believed that our culture, the American example, had to be put to an end, or if not, we earthlings were going to go the way of the Martians. The long, closely-held secret the government, the oil and car industries hid from the public, proved to them, once and for all, that the culture of greed could not be reformed, but had to be destroyed.

So why not a new Manhattan Project?

These people were a secret cabal of scientists from a small college in Vermont. During their sensational trial, all work stopped all across the world, as everyone sat riveted to our screens.

Who were these people who could kill so many of their fellow countrymen? What on earth could have possibly driven them so mad?

***

You have no idea how this act shook the collective consciousness of America, Father; more so then that incident in your time ever did. In the confusing, chaotic days and months following the bombing, even as I did my duty for my tank Battalion, I was numbed. And I saw the same numbness in the eyes and body language of the men and women who served with me. Even tough old Colonel Bird seemed to be walking around as if in a dream.

I looked in on him one night in his office and saw that he was in tears.

Sorry sir," I said. I was embarrassed at catching him in such a sorry state.

"Oh, come on in, Major," he said, looking up at me. A half-full quart of Jack Daniel sat before him. He spoke with almost a sound of relief that I had broken him out of the deep funk he was in.

He wiped his eyes with his hands. He did not return my salute.

"Have a drink," he said, motioning to the bottle of bourbon. I wasn't much of a bourbon man, too strong, too 20th Century for me. But out of respect, I sat down and poured myself a small one.

"Blackjack" was not what many would expect of an American tank Battalion Commander. He was small, Chinese, with tiny dark eyes. His family had been in this country since the 1840's, and he spoke with a distinct Southern accent.

He sat slumped over in his chair, looking smaller than usual.

He didn't have a loud voice, but there was something about him that could intimidate, and make his body and voice seem much larger than they really were. He could fill and command a room just by his being.

And he clearly loved the role that fate had so artfully dealt him as he strutted about, giving us orders, and telling us confidently how we ruled the world.

I once asked him how he got the name "Blackjack?"

He smiled at me, revealing little. He loved playing these kinds of mind games. "'Blackjack'" sounds like a real ass-kicker, don't it, Major?"

"Yeah, I would say so, sir. I would say so."

"Well the truth is, I play a mean game of blackjack. And poker. It's my Asian face."

The Colonel broke into a loud laugh. I had known him for three years, but never had I heard him laugh like this.

Now this new voice, a voice I had never heard before either, a voice I couldn't conceive coming from someone like him—a voice that was low, old, tried, shaken, confused.

He slowly wiped his dark eyes once again, and did not appear to be embarrassed by my catching him in tears.

During his real life, when we weren't playing at being military, he worked on Wall Street, and was very successful at what he did.

On that fateful day, as I walked the beach talking with Mother, he also couldn't bring himself to leave his stately, comfortable home in Bronxville and go into his office.

"I was just sitting there, talking to him on the DYE, talking to Larry, for Christ's sake. Good old Larry. We spent a year together at Old Miss. I transferred to The Point. He said, "you crazy, Bird!" We stayed in touch. Known him for so long. He ran the place really, Major. I'm running around the world with crazy folks like you. But good old Larry. I always wanted you two to meet. So much alike. Good old Larry. Arrogant bastard! Best-dressed man I ever knew. He was part black like you, Major.

"Said dressing was a black thing. What does that mean, Major? You know what the last thing he said to me just before the screen went black and he disappeared forever?"

"No sir," I answered.

"He said, 'That's an ugly damn robe you wearing, Bird!' Those were his last words. Arrogant bastard! I don't how many times I wanted to fire his arrogant ass. Had gray eyes, just like you have blue eyes. But I never did, Major. I never did. Arrogant bastard. Smart as all hell.

"For Christ's sake!"

I looked down at my glass, saying nothing. What could I say, Father? There was much despair in Colonel Bird's voice.

"I saw the flash, as far away as I was."

"I saw it as well, and I was all the way in Brighton Beach."

"Yes, it was really something, Major. The goddamn DYE just went blank and poor Larry just disappeared. Why do you think they did it, Major Litvinova? Why? Why kill so many people? You would have thought we learned something? Killing people like that only brings on more killing. They should know that? What do they want, Major?"

All who had witnessed the flash and the loud explosion wanted to talk about it to everyone we met more than anything else. So I understood, Father. I also knew that the Colonel's world had totally collapsed, more so than mine, although neither one of us knew what we were going to do next.

His office in Manhattan, like mine, was gone, reduced to nothing, along with good old Larry and hundreds of his friends and colleagues. He could have been there, arrogant, a good dresser, just like Larry; just as I could have been sitting at my desk, trying to think up yet another clever slogan, for yet another clever movie.

But there was a big difference between the two of us, Father. He was the king, the big fish, the real Master of The Universe, who strode mightily into his huge office with a look of great confidence and power, while I was a medium sized fish, still flirting on the edge of real power; close, but not quite there yet. A Major.

I had no answer for the Colonel. I felt slightly ashamed of myself. Maybe I would have had an answer if I only had paid a little more attention to those warners. Maybe we shouldn't have spent so much time in clubs, laughing and drinking, and having a great time? Maybe we should have read more books? Or any books.

"I don't know, sir. I really don't know," I finally answered. I keep staring at my drink, lost in as much confusion as the Colonel. But I no longer felt any embarrassment at sharing this quiet, no longer awkward moment with a strong man, an old friend, and a trusted colleague in the greatest army on earth. I felt honored to be sitting here with him this evening, sharing a drink together.

I knew that we both felt small, weak and out of control of the very essences of our being.

Chapter 5

Thank God for the army, Father. At least it gave my life shape and meaning for the months we searched desperately for someone to attack.

Now look at them, Father! Our formidable enemy! Capable of killing millions in a single blow. Capable of bringing almost to a standstill, not only the mightiest nation the world had ever seen, but the entire world itself—a bunch of nondescript college professors from Vermont.

Colonel Bird never had a chance to see who it was that destroyed his life. He blew his brains out shortly after our outfit returned to reserved status.

He took a shiny, silver, old fashion Army issued Colt 45, that his father, a retired Tanker, a Brigadier, had given him when he graduated from West Point, and spattered bone, blood and gray matter all over his bedroom.

His neatly pressed, dress Army uniform, complete with the yellow ribbon of the mighty Calvary, and all the many medals he had won, was totally ruin.

In our first and only real "Trial of The Century" we all watched closely these ordinary looking three white men and one lone woman, and just stared as closely as the television cameras would allow.

I won't bore you with all the details of the trial, Father. Or the endless horror stories of grief, broken lives and near total despair. Almost every single person in the country knew of someone who had died that day, or died days, or months later. It was if a large gray blanket had been thrown across the land.

Needless to say, the five were easily convicted, and promptly executed. But you know what, Father, they won. In the end, they had their day in court. They wanted to talk to the world. And they did, and the entire world listened. That was all they wanted. That was what all of this was all about.

They explained in cool, frightening detailed terms why they did what they did, and what they hoped would spring forth from their actions. And they were right; it was never the same again.

I remember this one guy because he was so different from the rest. He didn't speak calmly in a high-toned, professorial manner. He was tall, super-intelligent, a little on the fat side. He had large bulging, light blue eyes, and an unruly halo of blond hair. He seemed barely able to breathe as he testified; as if he was hyperventilating. Even through the television you could make out little beads of sweat coming from his forehead. He spoke in rapid spurts of complicated words.

He was clear about one thing, however:

"We had one wake-up call this century, but we didn't wake up, but allowed the money class to once again take over our lives, and push dumb movie stars, and non-thinking on us—as if we were all stupid idiots—as they raped the world. Martin Luther King would have done the same thing," he insisted.

Martin Luther King? I was appalled, Father. How dare he! More like that nut case I heard about, Timothy McVeigh, or that other guy, the Unabomber.

But, as I said, they won, and the change they hoped for, and killed millions of people to achieve, came slowly, but it came nevertheless. So much of what we were as a nation had been centered on that small island we called Manhattan. So much history. So much human knowledge, despite the redundancies built after Sept.11—was lost. One by one, all of the important institutions that kept America afloat were going from bad to worse.

We then elected this one guy who was going to lead us back to the promise land. It was a promise land alright.

Chapter 6

Shall I once again take another short little break from all of this gloom and doom and Big Bang stuff, and tell you more about how life was for Mother and me once we settled in Brooklyn, Father?

Ok, let's talk about Mother. You want to know more about what life was like in Brighton Beach for Mother. We found a great place a half-a-block from the beach at 3099 Brighton 6 Street on the fifth floor over looking the street.

You know that by now she was a mature woman in her fifties, with brand new front teeth and all. Her cousin immediately found her a job in a Russian bookstore near where we lived, and she could walk to work. That was the first big blessing: no more cars, with their expensive gas, constant breakdowns and watchful cops always on the prowl. Mother rarely got political about anything, but she always thought the politicians in LA needed to be put in jail for not providing adequate public transportation.

Soon she started to regain her old confidence. This is where I first understood the power of art. It was art, Father! That was your great insight into what made some of us so different. Sergie couldn't take it away from her. The lost of you, her precious black American Pushkin couldn't take it away. This strange, artless country couldn't take it away.

An artist is always an artist, until they die. And yes, she was an artist, you once wrote about her.

And how right you were, Father. She founded a theatre company dedicated to the Russian classics, which were performed only in Russian. The Pushkin Playhouse, she grandly named it, in honor of both her only son, and the great Pushkin of Mother Russia.

I remember her taking me to this small storefront at 259 Brighton 2 Street, right off of busy Brighton Beach Avenue. I could still see the old sign of its former business. It was barely readable. It read: Barber Shop.

"See, Alex," Mother said. "Need work."

Need work indeed! I worked with Mother for months helping get the theater in shape. The inside looked like it had not been occupied in years, and had a stale, funny smell. In the end, the theater was small potatoes, but it kept her busy and made her happy. She loved being on stage, as you well know, Father. But now, she was not only acting, but she also tried her hand at directing.

And, as you have undoubtedly guessed by now, I grew up fluent in Russian. After you died that was almost all we spoke in our apartment. That's why I could give the finger to people like David who dared question my Russian bona fide's.

After you left us, my Russian grew stronger and stronger. I guess Mother needed to talk to me. Mother said that one of the reasons she missed you so much was that you were quite the talker.

"All time, Alex," she would say, making the shape of two lips flapping together with her hands.

It seemed that all your talking greatly improved her English. But now that she was in Brighton Beach, surrounded by Russians speaking Russian, her English slipped, and all I heard in our apartment was mostly Russian.

I also spent a great deal of time in her little 40 seats, storefront theatre. Father, I don't know how much you saw her work. Here's what you wrote in your famous short story, *The Queen of Macy's:*

It was a surprising first meeting. I thought that I had met her before, many, many times. We shared the same work place, and met at least three times a week, and had spent long hours together, selling underwear, lounge wear and pajamas to The Valley elite, and world famous faces.

But this was the first time we had really met.

She had just revealed to me that she was a trained actress, and had what we in America would call a master's degree.

"Really," I said, very much surprised at this news.

"In Russia we must educate to work on stage," she answered carefully in broken English. I could see her face turn serious as she struggled to find just the right words.

"Well, what kinds of things did they teach you?" I asked. I now apprised her more closely; again, meeting the real her for the very first time after all these weeks.

"First," she said, all at once bending down in front of me, catching me somewhat off guard, twisting her body into a deformed shape, which made her seem like a broken down, defeated old lady.

A sad, downtrodden look appeared on her now weary face. "You don't play the king like this."

She suddenly straightened up, and all at once a profound transformation took place. Sasha held her thin body up regally, threw her blond head back in a haughty, lordly, disdainfully proud manner, and flashed me a youthful smile.

She then dramatically, theatrically threw out both of her hands.

"You play the king like this! For no matter what, the king is always the king." She then spread her arms out gracefully and took a small bow. She had a triumphant look on her face. Sasha's small, dark blue eyes were now huge, sparkling with life, and filled with great confidence.

All at once she was ten years younger, not the 39-year-old unhappy immigrant woman I thought I knew; and while not quite a king, Sasha was at the very least, a queen.

A few days later she brought in several stories that were written about her back in Russia.

I could not read Russian, but from the photo accompanying one story, I saw a younger version of her with a distracted look on her face, posing half nude, with a man leaning over her, seemingly in deep heat.

"We considered, how you say, avante garde. Yes, avante garde. I all the time in the newspapers. My director was sooo famous. Everyone in Moscow knew him," she said.

We both stared long and hard at her former self. I saw a look of pure pride on her face, and also, almost a sense of disbelief that that beautiful young, daring looking woman in that black and white photograph, laying back on a couch in such an artful pose, was once her.

***

How wonderfully observed, Father. I wish I were as gifted as you were. I have read that passage quite a bit lately. I could picture both of you starting to realize each other's true self, coming to an awareness of each other's special ness. It has brought tears to my eyes many, many times.

But Father, did you ever really get a chance to see just how gracefully she moves on stage? If so, you would have noticed how she would wave her delicate hands around like a precious, human butterfly, and move across the stage tossing her head all about dramatically. It was at moments like these moments that I saw the magical powers she held in her small body; the power of The Muse.

It was hard to believe this was the same woman up there; my mother. She was still on the thin side, and she still had the old charm, the old magic, the same ability to turn men into adoring little puppy dogs, or brilliant creative artists, or mean, jealous, dangerous maniacs.

She had become involved with a Russian man I hated. I heard that he was a gangster, a member of the famous Russian Mafia. Needless to say, Father, that relationship only lasted for a few years. Not that the gangster, as I called him, wasn't nice to Mother.

It was clear even to me, that he absolutely adored her.

In fact, he largely financed that little 40 seat non-profit theatre. I know it was him who talked her into opening it, with promises of as much cash as she needed.

No, I didn't hate him because he was a crazy, abusive man like Sergie. He seemed like a nice person. He was soft spoken, with a strong Russian accent whenever he spoke in English, and he laughed a lot. It was hard to believe, as the whispers on the street had it, that he was a mean, callous, violent extortionist, drug dealer and hired killer.

Mother said that he had "courtly" old world manners. He was a thin, tall, brown-eyed Jew like Sergie. He was the first Jew Mother had met in America she liked. She hated the Jews she met in Los Angeles. "They not like Russian Jews. In Russia, Jews are funny and interesting. Not like here. They not real Jews."

The gangster was a real Jew for her, however. He was funny, and alive, and generous on top of it, and seemed to like Mother for her Muse-like qualities, which pleased her greatly. He never said much to me, almost as if I wasn't even around, as he directed all of his conversation toward Mother. He just grunted at me when he came over, and that served as the cue for me to go to my room and leave the two of them alone.

Still, I didn't like him. Maybe it was the thought that Mother was in the next room making love with him. I hate to tell you this, Father, but I once opened the door and saw Mother going down on him. Can you imagine! My mother!

Maybe my reaction to the gangster was the reaction of a jealous teenager, madly in love with his own mother? Or maybe I just didn't like the way he made his money, and the company he kept? I could see Mother drawn into a dangerous world of guns, drugs and who knows what else.

I knew what the word on the street was about him, and I became very nervous, and once pleaded with Mother to stop seeing him.

"Please Mother, please!" I begged her.

I was seventeen, and already, I towered over her, and I was still growing.

Tall or not, Mother could still quickly put me in my place, and intimidate me beyond belief. I had watched her on stage. I knew she could throw darts across the room better than anyone I had ever seen. Even through I knew she was an actress, still, when she whirled and fixed her small blue eyes coldly on me, the same blue eyes I had inherited—I was frozen in my place.

"Alexander," she answered sharply in a loud, high-pitched voice in Russian, "Just stop it! Just shut up!"

I was shocked! Mother rarely called me Alexander, and almost never yelled at me.

I was also taken aback because I saw the look of hurt on her face. That look said I was selfish. That I was trying to take away what little happiness and pleasure she got out of life. That I was a thoughtless ingrate. I knew what her face was telling me!

Father, I felt so ashamed and embarrassed. I felt that I had stuck my stupid, dumb nose into something I had no business. I quickly went to my room and closed the door.

I turned on the thin screen hanging on my wall and put on little dark goggles and immediately engrossed myself in a video game, struggling against mighty electronic foes that seemed as if they could reach out and knock me on my stupid, ungrateful ass.

I vowed never to bring up the subject again.

Well, it turned out Father that I didn't have to. A few months after my emotional confrontation with Mother, I was sitting in our living room, alone, watching a movie. It was Friday. It was late, past mid-night.

Mother had produced, starred in, and directed Anton Chekhov's *Uncle Vanya*. She played Mrs. Voynitsky with uncommon bravado.

The play was well received, and a local success; her first real success in her theatre after two grueling, frustrating years.

A local paper even ran her picture and a rave review of the play in it. They called her, and the Pushkin Playhouse, a local "cultural treasure." All of this attracted large crowds, as Old World Russians poured into the theater.

Mother had pulled it off, big time, Well, big time for her, Father.

I knew that Friday was always her best night, and that afterward, she and the gangster would go to dinner and stay out until early in the morning, hanging out in one of the many clubs where they had become local celebrities because of Mother's new found fame, and obviously, because everyone knew who he was.

And equally as obvious, I had mixed feeling about her new success. Suddenly I wasn't seeing much of my mother anymore!

But I was used to that by now. Whether I liked it or not, theater people, I have learned, are all night people. They start coming alive, just when other people are shutting down for the evening. They are not the kind of people that like sitting home at night watching television.

We lived of the fourth floor, and our living room, which also served as Mother's bedroom, faced the street.

Suddenly I heard loud screaming in Russian coming from the street below. One voice sounded like the gangster. I then thought I heard Mother's voice.

I ran to the window just in time to see someone being chased across the street by two men.

BANG! BANG! BANG!

Three shots rang out, and the chased man fell right in front of 3096. Lights went on all over the place! The two men ran, but not until one of them managed to pump two more shots into the man lying on the ground.

I was sure it was the gangster who was now lying bleeding to death. But where was Mother! Father? I never felt so scared before in my life. Was Mother dead? Were they now going to come and shoot me?

I heard someone fumbling at the door, which further scared the living shit out of me! I didn't know whether to run and open it, or put a chair in front of it to keep whoever it was out of my apartment!

I know I was thinking cowardly thoughts, Father, more afraid for my own safety than that of Mother's. I am deeply ashamed of myself, even now, as I write this, years later.

But it was Mother at the door, out of breath, Father.

She was flushed, sweaty, red-faced, frightened out of her wits! She had run up the entire flight of stairs, afraid to wait for the elevator, afraid that the assassins wanted her as dead as her now dead boyfriend.

But it wasn't her they wanted. They got what they wanted! He was lying in a pool of blood, right in front of our living room window.

Once again, Father, the now familiar crackling, and official sounding voices coming through the radios of the police, echoed loudly through our living room, as they did once before in Los Angeles.

"I know nothing! I know nothing!" Mother kept insisting, her Russian accent now becoming heavier. She started biting her bottom lip and glanced nervously around, throwing me quick, dart-like looks.

The two black policemen listened patiently, fiddled with their loud radios, and took long copious notes. They looked at Mother with suspicious, skeptical dark eyes, unlike the deep sympathy I had seen in the eyes of the white and Hispanic policewomen years ago.

Chapter 7

It was because of that event that I first met David. Then he was a 20-year-old writer, and already a graduate student at Columbia. He was a real genius. He wrote for a local paper, and lived near us in Brighton Beach.

He was also a Russian Jew, but like many of the Russian Jews in Brighton Beach, his family had been here since the turn of the last century.

He dogged Mother for weeks after the shooting trying to get an interview for an article he was doing on the Russian Mafia in Brighton Beach.

Of course Mother didn't talk to him, for obvious reasons. For one, she was now one of the most notorious people in Brighton Beach, and not because she was a "cultural treasure,"

Talk about up and downs, Father. Just as soon as she had put her little theatre on the map, and established herself as an artistic force, all at once, overnight, she transformed into a gangster's moll!

How unfair, Father! Can you imagine, this middle aged, 57-year-old single mom, with a half black Russian teenage son, a gangster's moll? I mean, Father, please!

Mother wouldn't talk to David, so he turned to me, and tried to pump me for information. He was a persistent bastard, to be sure. He wasn't fat as he became. But I would walk out of my house, and there he was.

Also, I know now that David wanted more from me than just a good story. Even as young and inexperience as he was as a reporter, surely he must have known that I knew little about The Gangster's life style other than he liked banging my mother.

I know now that what David really wanted was nothing more than to get down on his knees and give me a blowjob.

"P," he said later, after we had settled into real friendship, without the sex, based partly on our both growing up in Brighton Beach and being Russian, "when I first laid eyes on you, this tall, handsome, well-built, brown-skinned "Russian" with blue eyes no less, I knew I was gay! I said, 'that's it, no more women for me.'"

I laughed hardily, freely, at his kind words. David always loved putting a not so subtle emphasis on the word "Russian" as if I was some kind of bogus Russian. But I was more Russian than he will ever be, and he knew it!

Gina was with us that day, as we sat in one of our favorite clubs in Manhattan. She also laughed a quick, nervous laugh. Gina often looked confused at the close relationship, and open affection the two of us shared, with David always flirting with me. Sometimes I thought she really suspected that we were really getting it on.

"Get the fuck out of here, David. I made you gay? Is that what you're saying! I made you gay?" My voice was filled with playful, mock indignation. All three of us laughed loudly.

I didn't know he was gay back then. He just seemed like a nice guy, and although he was older than I was, I liked him immediately. In many ways, he became the older brother I never had.

Mother, however, never took so well to David. First, because he was a nosy reporter. "Don't you talk to him, Alex," she warned me more than once, narrowing her small eyes at me.

She didn't have to warn me so many times. I was the one who had seen The Gangster gunned down. You, Father, are perhaps the first person I am sharing this with. I never told Mother. I never told David. I never told the police what I saw that night out of my window.

Mother told the police that she had already entered the building when the shooting took place, and didn't see anything. She didn't tell them, which I had witness a part of, that when the two hit men approached both of them, her boyfriend instantly knew what was about to go down.

After a brief, but loud conversation, which I had overheard, Mother saw one of the men pull out a gun.

"Run Sasha!" The Gangster shouted.

Mother ran into the building as he started running across the street, drawing the men away from her, and allowing her to get safely away. He saved her life, for in all probability, if he hadn't run in the direction he did, they both would have been gunned down. It was clear he was thinking of her safety as he ran, sealing his death. He knew they wanted him, not her.

Thank God, Father, Mother didn't see The Gangster gunned down; she was too busy running up the long flight of stairs.

She had never seen the two men who shot her boyfriend before. Again, word on the street was busily buzzing away. Some said that they were imported from California. Other's said they came from Israel. Still other's said they came directly from Moscow. The police never caught them, which cause much fear in both Mother and myself. We both knew that she had fully seen their faces when they confronted The Gangster and her of the street.

What was unspoken in the back of both of our minds was would they now come after her because she could identify them? The Russian didn't play. We both knew that. Everyone in Brighton Beach knew that! Dead bodies popped up everywhere, including old people, women, and even children, when someone was pissed-off.

When all is said and done, Brighton Beach is like a small town. And like in any small town, if you knew something that could put a hurting on the powers-that-be, you kept your mouth shut if you wanted to stay alive.

Talking to someone like David would have been beyond foolish, Father. Both Mother and I walked the streets of Brighton Beach for months looking over our shoulders. I even had a nightmare that some strange guy, with crazed, blazing eyes suddenly burst through the large crowd of shoppers and strollers on the big Avenue and pointed a large gun at Mother.

"Run, Shasa! Run, Shasa!" someone yelled.

I forced myself to wake up before the madman had a chance to kill Mother. She was right. The last thing we needed was to have our name and pictures in the papers talking about the Russian Mafia!

Mother soon closed the Pushkin Playhouse.

I asked her why. She avoided my eyes.

"Alex, theatre doesn't make money. How am I supposed to pay the rent? You got money?"

I wish I did have money, Father. I felt so sorry for her, because I knew how much being on stage meant to her. She couldn't do American theatre because of her heavy accent, and her still limited ability to read English. I also knew that although money was a problem, especially now that her deep-pocketed boyfriend was dead—it had always been a problem, but that didn't stop her in the past.

I knew she was now filled with a deep fear, and a great lost. That she just didn't have the heart anymore, and did not want to be out late.

She even started transferring that fear to me. After that shooting, she started getting on my case whenever I was late coming home. She started clinging to me, Father, which bothered the holy hell out of me.

One of the things I loved growing up with an actress, an artist—as you probably loved because you were also an artist—was her sense of independence and purpose in life. Everyday living with such a person had meaning. They were not just going through life sleeping, working, consuming and following orders.

Mother was a great role model. She gave a kid like me a freer range than most kids.

But this insane killing was taking away this freedom, Father. Now it was: Alex this! And Alex that! And Alex don't do this! Alex, don't go over there! Alex, Alex, Alex!

No wonder I joined the Army as soon as I left college.

The Gangster's death, and her own close brush with death, clearly shook her, Father.

Chapter 8

Of all the things that you wrote, Father, other than what you wrote about Mother, one passage has always stood out in my mind. I have it underlined in yellow and maybe for reasons of age, a greater understanding and respect for thought and contemplation, or just the sheer pride that my father wrote such wise words, I go back to it often lately.

In your last novel you had one of your characters say, *"Life is mysterious, scary…with no rhyme or reason. There's not one person on this planet that knows with absolute certainty what it's all about. Not one, despite all the bullshit. So, why hurt people, even if they are your enemy? Why go out and deliberately try to hurt another human being? Life itself will sooner or later give them all the hurt that they will ever need. Why add to their misery?"*

With all due respect, Father, at first when I first read it I said bullshit. It sounded good, but it was still bullshit. As a man of action, a Major in the mighty tank Corp, a mover and shaker in the business world of Manhattan, I was more than ready to put a hurting on anyone who tried to hurt me or someone close to me, and give them as much misery as they gave me.

But as I've aged and bore full witness to the awful pain of the world of the living—from losing my dear friends from the Big Bang, and notwithstanding the awful pain Mother experienced, first from losing you, her brilliant, loving Pushkin; to the gruesome pain, both physical and mental that Sergie inflicted on her; the cold-blooded terror of witnessing the death of the Gangster; to the disappointment of the so-called American dream—I understood why you wrote what you wrote.

You wrote that in your late fifties. I doubt very much if you could have written the same words even ten years earlier. I now know that those are the wise words of an older person who has lived long enough, felt deeply enough, and cared strongly enough that he profoundly understands much of the real pain of life.

***

After that wild night in Brighton Beach of the shooting of The Gangster, things became very quiet for us. I finished high school and worked my way through Brooklyn College, mainly by joining the ROTC.

Also, Father, you'll be happy to know, we received a little money from the sales of your books. A steady little drip, drip, drip. Mother's eyes would light up every time she opened her mailbox and there stood an unexpected check from your last publisher.

It's a good thing you understood copyright laws and taught Mother how to protect your works.

"See, Alex," she said once, putting the thin check right in front of my nose, "He kept saying, 'you are so beautiful, sooooo lovely. I love kissing your lips, so I give you something, I give you intellectual property. I leave you intellectual property. Worth more than gold.'

'I say, hon, give me gold; you keep your intellectual property!'"

Mother laughed merrily in a loud, high-pitched voice and started happily dancing around our apartment, still waving your little gift from the grave around with her small little hands.

Her memories of you are so fond, Father! I didn't have the heart, or the nerve, to say to her, "I guess Father was right, his intellectual property is worth more than gold."   Your novels, except one, the notorious, The Woman's Man, tanked, so to speak. But your book of essays became somewhat of an American classic and is still being taught at colleges across the country and overseas. You got the last laugh on all those doubters, Father, and left me, Mother, and the world a very real part of you, and much wisdom.

I must say this, however. That book of yours also brought me some grief when I was at Brooklyn College. Although I do not share your last name, the word soon got out that I was your son. Those guys in the Black Studies Department thought that because of who I came from, I should show a little more racial consciousness and solidarity.

I took a class from this one guy who loved your book and taught it in his class on Black Intellectual Thought in the 20th Century. But boy, Father, was he a pain in the ass! He was a bearded asshole with little dreadlocks. And it was black this, black that, and he was always putting down white people. And Father, he seemed like he was always pointing a finger at me as to what was wrong with the black race.

But, what the fuck was I supposed to do, Father? Hate Mother, for Christ sake?

The bastard ended up giving me a C! Can you believe that shit? A fuckin' C? But, at least he thought you were one of America's greatest intellectual heroes, even if you did have a half-ass Russian son.

But all that black shit, who needed it?

Instead, I defied the black study crowd and dated white and Asian girls, studied military history and business, danced, happily jerking myself around spastically to white boy bands, and called myself a Russian.

Shame on me, Father!

***

But poor, dear Mother? I don't think she ever had another boyfriend after The Gangster. At least I never saw her with anybody. And she never stepped foot back on stage after that crazy night. She immediately closed the play down, closed the theatre, and ended her career as an actress/director.

Now she just fussed and worried herself on my behalf. She was so proud the day I received my degree. Her little blue eyes just beamed with great joy.

At least, Father, she had that one shining, brilliant moment in the American spotlight, if only in little Brighton Beach, at a small 40 seat theatre bringing artistic life once again to Uncle Vanya.

***

Meanwhile, back to the Big Bang. As to be expected, everyone demanded that something be done to change the course of this country.

Money and Big Capital had leaded us down a road to ruin. Of course, this threw our political process into turmoil.

President Bush had less than two years to go in his second term and there were strong voices coming from all over the country demanding drastic changes in the way the country and businesses were run.

And there was this one unsuspected voice that became the strongest of all. His name was Jerry M. Guess, Jr. and he was an AME preacher from Columbia, South Carolina. And this cat was homely, Father. I mean homely, with big thick glasses and buckteeth.

Since the advent of television, it has been the conventional wisdom that only good-looking people could run for President.

Certainly President Bush was a very handsome man. His hair was still full, and it had turned a mixed steel gray and black. His mother was a Mexican, and his father was a pudgy-looking old line WASP. Somehow he managed to look both Mexican and Anglo, with his brown eyes and wide, full tooth smile.

In many ways, for the people who thought about such things, they considered him the best television President ever. Even better than his uncle, George the Second, and certainly better than his grandfather, George the First!

It has also been conventional wisdom that no dark skin—especially true if he is a down home, bible thumping black male from the Deep South—could ever be elected President.

But that was before The Big Bang. The Big Bang, along with our worsening weather and the realization that Americans were willing to kill each other in numbers larger than any outside enemy had, made us all a little crazy.

I mean, why not, Father? First, we find out that our business and political leaders were slowly, deliberately poisoning us to death for profit. Then we find out that we are really Martians! Then our own citizens, for God sakes, nuked us! That's enough to drive anybody crazy!

What have we become, was the unanswered question. I know I asked that question over and over. I was so lonely, so very lonely, I could barely stand it. Now that I was no longer chasing shadows, trying to find bad guys, I didn't know what to do with myself anymore.

I was back home, out of uniform, and the grim reality of my new life started to unfold slowly before me. This meant that I could no longer pick up the phone, call David, and talk to him hours on end. It meant I couldn't hold and fuck my cute little Gina. I couldn't hang with the gang in those great Manhattan bars. I couldn't go to my neat little office and wait until quitting time to hit the clubs and meet my friends.

Things had changed a great deal since your day, Father.

My generation rediscovered a good time, at least in the Big Apple. That was our thing. I know you railed in your essays about the long hours of work that young people put in at the turn of the century. But, fuck that, Father! They were real assholes! You were right! That was one lesson we learned, all right.

We knew how to party and have a good time. Oh, we worked hard. I'm not saying that we didn't work hard. We were no slackers, by any means, Father. But work was not the end all for us, which It was for young people in your day. Everyone now looked back on that time as a strangely bizarre time!

Maybe we learned something from the workaholic generation that came before us. Work for Generation Rule was just that—work! It was something to give you some money to do what you really wanted to do, which was to hang out, drink, talk shit, have a good time, get as much sex as you could, and have a ball! Why the French still hated us so much is beyond me. In many ways, we had become a lot like them.

Maybe it was because they found a cure for AIDS, or legalized drugs, or had approved gay marriages, or maybe it was just Generation Rule's protest against the excesses of the last generation. The circle thing, as David might say.

***

I wasn't having a ball now after the Big Bang. I just quietly walked the beach in all kinds of weather, avoiding the eyes and nods of others, keeping a very private space, talking to Mother, talking to David, talking to you, Father; talking to all of those friends I had lost.

I remember one walk in particular. It was cold beyond belief. I was the only one foolish enough to be out on such a day. The wind was howling bitterly and stinging me with intense bursts of sudden pain with its relentless fury.

The gray Atlantic Ocean pounded beside me, loudly, viciously.

I had on a hooded jacket with a long topcoat over that. Even that was not enough to protect me from this brutal weather. I wanted to turn back, but didn't. I knew that I was punishing myself deliberately. I was filled with survivor guilt.

I had just resigned my commission. What good was being a Major in the so-called mighty Army if I couldn't even protect my friends, or at least avenge their death, Father?

After my friend and mentor, Colonel Bird blew himself to bits, the remainder of my love for the tank corp. quickly faded, just drained right out of me. I knew I was next in line for promotion and would have been made a Lt. Colonel and taken full command of my outfit...

But after eight years full time, and 12 years in the Reserves, it was over for me. After seeing my lifeless, brave friend lying so peacefully in his casket, his slim face a ghostly pale white, yet strangely serene; the mortician had done an excellent job of patching him up so that we could all pay out last respects. I paused a moment at his casket and stared long and hard at him. I remembered all the pain and unbearable suffering I saw in his face the last time I saw him alive—that's when I knew, Father. That's when I knew.

But on this cold bitter, angry day, it was not the military on my mind. The deed was done. I had quit. There was no turning back. I knew that. This day instead, it was the thought of death that was on my mind, Father, as I headed to the Fisherman's pier at Coney Island.

I could feel the tears freezing as they tried to run down my face, as I bent my head down into the furious wind. I finally made it to the end of the pier and watched as the high waves reached onto it, wetting my feet with their numbing cold.

I wished as mightily as I could that one would come and sweep me away. A huge, gigantic wave. One that would swiftly, decisively, carry me out into the cold deep and draw me under in a deadly embrace, where I would join my dead friends and my dead parents, and be whole again.

I shuttered violently, but not from the cold. I now felt real fears overtaking me, and it scared me like nothing I had ever experienced before. The specter of doom drew me away from the cold, angry water.

I looked death directly in the face that bitter winter day, Father, but I blinked.

I turned and ran off the pier to the empty boardwalk as fast as I could, with desperation and deep feeling of dread in my steps. I finally made it back to my apartment, frozen, sneezing and colder than I have ever been in my life. My feet were so frozen that I could hardly walk, and they pulsated with pain. I stayed in bed for almost a week after that, with the worst cold I ever had in my life!

I now knew that I didn't want to die, no matter how much guilt, shame, helplessness, loneliness, fear, anger and self-doubt I felt. But like most Americans, I now desperately wanted someone to tell me what went wrong? Where did we start walking the wrong path? What could we now do? What was to become of us? What was next?

Chapter 9

Well, what was next was that tall, dark-skinned, lanky, AME preacher from Columbia, S.C. named Rev. Guess, I told you about.

At first, everybody laughed. I was still following the news then and I watched the shirks of the smart-ass Generation Rule commentators when they discussed Rev. Guess. You had pushy, fearless black Reverends like that back in your day, Father. You even deftly portrayed one in your novel The Woman's Man. What was his name, the Rev. Alex?

If I was still hanging out in my bars in Manhattan with the gang, I could see us now, pointing at the large thin screen, laughing our hip, sophisticated, knowing laughter.

And me, the Major, the man of action, the mad Russian, would yell above the rest, "Get the fuck outta here!"

But Father, America was a land in deep psychological turmoil and pain. We could still make money better than everyone else. We still made things. Our military was still intact. Our businesses, as usual, made an amazing recovery. We still had more than we could eat. It was just that we didn't believe in very much.

Rev. Guess had an uncanny, almost supernatural ability to tap into, and probe our psychic pain. It was as if he had been sent from another world. His message was simple: moral decay.

I can see you smiling a thin, wry little smile now, Father. That message is as old as people. So-called religious and political leaders have been beating humans upside the head with that message since the first African grunted!

But this homely looking guy, as he peered into our living rooms, with his dark shining eyes visible behind his small, old-fashioned glasses, just seemed to be saying all of the things most people wanted to hear. He was the most eloquent person I had ever heard in my life.

God, Father, did he ever have a silver tongue! Let me give you an example:

"Did all our great wealth, our unparalleled military might, in the end, protect those millions who died that day? No!

"But what was New York City at the time of the Big Bang? What had it become? What made the All Mighty turn his gracious back on that den of evil? Yes evil, my fellow Americans.

"I don't want to cast blame on the dead, God rest their unfortunate souls, but the New York of 2037 was a hedonist place that denied all of God's basic rules. It was a place were there were more bars, more drugs, more men living with men, more women living with women, then men and women living in family, in harmony with nature, as God intended.

"More! More! More! More! More of everything that is wicked and evil in the world! They even had the nerve, the sheer, unmitigated gall, and the audacity to call themselves Generation Rule. Generation Rule? Rule what? Rule whom? Didn't they know in all of their arrogance, that only God rules? Generation Rule, indeed!"

He phased and stared at us; letting his words sink in, watching us closely through our television screens "And we wonder why, my fellow Americans" he concluded," that God turned his back on New York!"

This obviously didn't play well in what was left of New York. But for the rest of the country, Rev. Guess had turned into a national hero. A man of faith. A man of moral values. A man who believed deeply in something other than making a buck and poisoning people!

There was also an interesting sub-text to all of this, although unspoken. Rev. Guess was so attractive because he wasn't slick, well-package, official, press savvy—all of the things we had come to expect from our leaders of whatever color. Those qualities were now seen as the very things that had led us down this path of destruction and fear of the future. He was giving plainspoken, hard working, do all the grunt work Americans-- back a future.

What he gave me, Father were the creeps!

It seemed that he was making a direct attack on my friends and me; that somehow we were the ones that were responsible for the blast. I knew many people in the country hated and envied us in New York. We seemed to be the only ones having any fun.

America's children couldn't wait to dump those dull-ass suburbs and wannabe cities like that phony Dallas, or those boring small towns, and head for the exciting New York City. I mean, Father, it's always been hard to find a place to live in New York.

Just before the Big Bang it was outrageous! Someone estimated that over 25 per cent of the American population lived in the greater New York area, with most wanting more than anything to live in New York proper.

That's the real reason I stayed in Mother's apartment. There was no way I was going to pay $12,500 for a tiny studio anywhere in Manhattan! Even the Bronx was ridiculous. And Staten Island,

FORGETABOUTIT!

It seemed like the whole damn country, indeed the world, wanted nothing more than to be in New York. You talk about a city roaring back! It was a grand time to be here, Father. Maybe that's why bastards like Rev. Guess hated us so. In many ways, he was like those creeps that set off that bomb.

We had robbed them of their best and brightest. We had proven that big cities could work. That we didn't need their prayers and guilt trips. Rule and have a good time doing it! That was our motto. That's why they hated us, Father.

I only wished that David were around so I could ask him what he thought about the good Reverend.

"Can you imagine this crazy man!" I would ask incredulously. David would immediately know how disgusted I was because my tough guy New York street voice would become fully developed.

David would phase slightly, the way he always did, giving my question, or statement, as the case may be, careful consideration.

"Well, P," he would answer in his soft, almost feminine voice, "as a student of American history, you know that we are a circular society."

Ah yes, David's famous circle.

"What do you mean?" I would ask, as if I hadn't heard this theory many, many times.

"Ideas. Notions about who and what we are as a people. Every thirty years or so, usually kicked off by some event, like an assassination, a war, or a depression we go back to a set of old, discarded ideas. All the Rev. is doing is recycling the 80's and 90's, and he is right on time, P."

Of course I couldn't have that conversation with my thoughtful friend. He was now returned to the stardust from which we all came. But as I walked the beach, I imagined that was what he would have said.

It sounded just like him, Father.

But what about Mother. What would she have said about all of this? I doubt she would have said very much. In fact, she probably would have liked the Rev. Guess and gladly join his cause, and become one of his "Army of God."

After she gave up on men and the theatre, she began going to the local Russian Orthodox Church every week, and sometimes during weeknights. I would sometimes walk out of my bedroom and see her in the living room down on her knees, deep in prayer.

Even then, Father, she was still filled with high drama and was up to her old, colorful theatrics. Suddenly our apartment started smelling of heavily perfumed incense, and burning candles, and filling up with strange, mysterious looking religious icons which cast strange flickering black shadows on the walls whenever the lights were dimmed, and the candles lit.

It was the large black Madonna that really got my attention, however. Now that was really theatrical! Where she found it she never told me, maybe in what was left of black Harlem.

She would also warn me darkly to stay away from people like David.

"Don't argue with me, Alex. Against God," she said. She raised a bony finger at me censoriously. I had made the unfortunate mistake of asking her why she didn't want to catch David in our apartment ever again.

"Against God? What are you talking about, Mother?"

She just looked at me with her small blue eyes and shook her head. "You know what I mean, Alex!"

That was the end of that conversation! And David never set foot in our place again until Mother died. She had spent almost her entire life in the theatre, where damn near every man is gay; now, in her religious years, she didn't want her only son anywhere near people like that.

Yes, Father, I knew what Mother meant!

Mother would try to drag me to church with her, but I thought those Russian Orthodox priests, with their funny looking pointed hats, were as strange and medieval looking as the similarly dressed Ultra Orthodox Jews who were still a large part of New York City. People sure knew how to look as different from others as possible back in the days when those religions came under the complete control of a ruling class. Much like the army,

But I'm just thinking out loud, Father. Who knows why they one day decided to dress like that?

Whatever the case, Mother might have been right at home with Rev. Guess with his gay bashing, and fun bashing.

And you, Father? Who knows what you would have made of all of this?

***

Needless to say, Rev. Guess became all of the rage, and his "People's Army of God," blacks, whites, Hispanics, Asians, native people, the whole damn shebang, except of course the Jews and Muslims. And this is an interesting intersection of history, Father. Now these two bitter enemies were faced with even greater enemies.

As I said at the beginning of this letter, life as you knew it, stood on its head.

Still, with the Jews and Muslims standing on the sidelines, with no one paying any attention anymore to them, the world had never seen this kind of mass frenzy in a long, long time. The last time this occurred was in Nazi Germany, if my limited knowledge of history is correct. You should have seen it, Father.

Guess was swept into office on the Republican ticket of all things, in 2040. His extra long coattails pulled in many like-minded individuals at the national, state and local level. He and his movement was a phenomenon unmatched in American History

Our friends in the rest of the world, at first yawned and looked at us with growing bemusement. They had had their share of the Rev. Guess's of the world. Who did we think we were to have escaped such lunatics for so long!

"It's about time!" they seemed to say.

But I was appalled, Father.

Chapter 10

This was a terrible time for me, Father. The Rev. Guess years are still a big blur. I remember little, only noticing now and then, the passing of yet another restricted law.

Women were quickly tossed out of the military. Gay marriages were banned. People who got caught even carrying as much as one joint, were thrown in jail for years.

The clerics had taken over. Rev. Guess' entire cabinet was one big congregation of religious leaders.

Father, you wouldn't have recognized this America! For the first time in our history, we had more people leaving than coming in. No one with good sense wanted to come to America, which was just fine with Rev. Guess and his boys.

Along with gays, and women not staying home and raising their kids, and having the right to murder the unborn, they laid much of the blame for America's fall from grace on the corruption of "foreign influence."

Soon, the sneering stopped. The rest of the world started getting very nervous. Rev. Guess was no longer a comic figure to be snickered at, but was gaining by the day, more and more power, and was armed to the teeth with nukes and the best military hardware in the world. The world knew that America was on a hair-trigger and one false move by anyone meant a sure attack.

But I could have cared less by all the politics. I had gradually withdrawn into a harden shell, which became harder, and harder until I totally withdrew from the world. Politics had become vague, although I knew instinctively that I was living in a world now more dangerous than anything that you could have imagined, Father.

Still, I didn't care what happened to the world. Let them all die, like my friends had died! I just walked the beach unshaven, often talking out loud to Mother, and David, and Gina, and my leader, Colonel Bird.

I hung on for dear life to Mother's apartment. I supported myself mainly from my pension from my Army service. Rev. Guess was smart enough not to piss off us Vets. In fact, he even increased the amount of money we received.

He even went on the air and made the announcement. This is what he said to the nation. And this is the last time I ever listened to anything he had to say:

"We have had an effete elite that was willing to fight to the last black, Hispanic and hard working poor white, but they and their children wouldn't be caught dead in a uniform. They just saw war as a means to money and power for themselves, and people like them. The rest of us were just cannon fodder.

"They never witnessed the dying. They never saw buddies being blown to tiny pieces. They never saw dead citizens piled on top of each other like hogs in a slaughterhouse. They stayed back in the comfort of their plush offices in New York and Washington and wrote articles and books, and gave expensive speeches, urging us on to fight their battles.

"War was just a big theory for them. And those bloodsuckers became richer and richer off the fallen blood of our countrymen. People like those deserve our contempt, and do not even deserve citizenship, much less the elite status they once enjoyed in this country. Well those days are over! We will reward those brave men who are willing to put their life on the line. They are the true elite!"

That Guess fellow was sure a hot number wasn't he, Father! You can imagine how resentful Middle America applauded those lines. I even clapped, for Christ sakes. They can keep their phony thank you for you service, bullshit. Give us Goddamn money, assholes! Go on Rev. Guess!

But that was the last time I ever listened to a political speech.

***

The other source of income also came from the Government in the form of disability payments.

It seemed that those of us that could have been killed that day, but for some reasons were spared, suffered much mental anguish afterward. We now have our own little category of mental illness: "The Manhattan Syndrome" as it is officially called.

It was recognized that people like us could no longer function as we once did. We were filled with too much pain. So we were paid our little bit of money each month, but on the condition that every month we visit our assigned shrink. They wanted to make it twice a month, but there was so much protest that they made in monthly.

The major reason why we protested, and most of us hated with a passion going to those witch doctors, was because we felt that we had become lab animals, curiosity pieces.

My first doctor was Dr. Francine Anderson, a forty-eight year old Ph.D. Dr. Anderson was clearly fascinated by what goes on in the mind of someone who have experience such total, irreversible loss.

She would greet me in her office in downtown Newark in the same manner, month after month. For some reason, Father, Newark had become the new Manhattan.

"How are we feeling, Major Litvinova," she would unfailing ask.

With Dr. Anderson it was always how were "we" feeling, as if the pain, hurt, fear, loss and deep depression I carried around with me, was also her pain, her lose.

She was nowhere near Manhattan when the bomb went off. She then lived and worked in Chicago, and rarely, if ever, came to New York.

She once quietly confided in me, bending her face so close to mine that I smelled her breath, becoming so intimate, probably as a ploy to gain my confidence, and maybe open me up a bit, that when the government announced this program on our behalf—she couldn't wait to be a part of it. "The team," as she put it.

It's a chance of a lifetime," she said.

Dr, Anderson wasn't bad looking. In fact she looked fairly attractive for a woman her age. She was of average size, and looked to be in fairly good shape. She was blond, and she looked like she came from a highly privileged background.

You know what I mean, Father? You've seen people like that. They just look rich for some reason.

I didn't know if she was rich or not. We never discussed that. In fact, we never discussed much of anything.

I spent most of my time with her muttering little "yes" or "no," or "maybe you're right," as she pressed and probed me. I really didn't want to talk to her, despite her seemingly open manner. No matter how many times she said "we" I knew she wasn't talking about her and me. She could never begin to understand my pain. No matter what I told her, how could she even begin to understand what it felt like to see a gay, happy world completely disappear, never to be seen or heard from again.

What did she know of that, Father?

A few months before she finally gave up on me, she snapped and started yelling at me in a very unprofessional manner, for being such a weenie

"For God's sakes, Major Litvinova! I know your service record! I read it. You're a brave man. You had a command vehicle shot from under you, but you were able to pull several to safety, while risking your own life. They gave you a Silver Star for that! You were one of the tough guys. You have looked death in the face, but you have always come through, and showed great leadership.

"So show some leadership now, Major! Show some leadership, damn it! Tell me how you are feeling about all this. How can I help you if you won't talk to me?"

Despite this emotional outburst, I still kept looking away, still locked deeply in my own private space.

Dr. Anderson suddenly started crying in sheer frustration.

"I'm so sorry, Major. That was so unprofessional of me. I apologize, Major Litvinova. I apologize."

Dr. Anderson reached over and took both of my hands into her's and placed them gently beside her left cheek. I could feel the warm tears against my hands. But what could I say to her, Father. What could I say that could make her feel better?

Chapter 11

"**A**ren't you Sasha Litvinova's son?" the young woman asked me. She looked me directly in my face, and did not seem at all put off by my unshaven, withdrawn look.

Father, talk about a shock to my system! Who the hell was this person? And how did she know Mother? And why was she speaking to me? I was just sitting on this bench minding my own damn business!

But can you believe it, Father, those five little words changed the course of my life forever, and lifted me out of seventeen long, lonely years of despair and desperation,

It was April 17, 2054, a little after one in the afternoon. I am not quite sure about the time, just the date; still, I thought it was a little after one, mainly because I did the same thing, at the same time, every day that the weather allowed—which was to sit and stare at the ocean, and occasionally take one of my walks to Coney Island and back.

The so-called Manhattan Syndrome still had me firmly in its deadly grip. I didn't own a DYE. I can't remember the last time I read a newspaper, or anything. I was plugged into nothing! Absolutely nothing.

Except one thing. Listen to this Father, remember that old rack set you had, with CD, radio, tape and vinyl all combined. I still have it! Can you believe that shit! Nothing on it works anymore, but of all things, the turntable. That old turntable works just fine.

That's my only passion. I search everywhere, looking for those old vinyl records. I will trek anywhere if I hear about how I could get my hands on these precious treasures.

Recently, I even took a boat trip to the Bronx because a dealer told me about a place that still sold vinyl. But I shouldn't have taken that trip, Father.

As we slowly churned our way up the East River, I didn't want to go there, but something drew me, some ghost whispered to me, Father, and I couldn't help myself.

I walked outside and felt the cool air hit me. I turned and looked at that huge pile of hot rubble and the ghostly shells of burned out buildings. I knew all my friends would remain buried forever underneath all that crap.

As strange as it may seem, Father, I had avoided this scene all of these years. This was the very first time I was viewing it in person. I had only seen it on screen, or whenever I flew over it, when I was in the military, or in print. But I never went up to look for myself, until this trip to the Bronx.

I stared long and hard as we slowly passed the once grand island of Manhattan. It was unbelievable! I mean, unbelievable, Father!

I soon noticed an older white couple staring with the same disbelief. Most of the younger people on deck had grown up with it and were paying that still smoldering big junk heap little mind. They just kissed, hugged and laughed with each other, reminding me of another time.

Just as I knew little about Sept. 11th, these young people knew nothing of all the grand buildings that once stood so proudly, that once helped define who we were as a country, grand buildings that once reached so high to the sky, so mighty, so world conquering, that all the world wondered in jealous awe!

Now it was gone!

The older couple started holding each other tightly, with the woman burying her head in his shoulder, as the old man gently patted her on her back. I could see her elderly body shaking. I watched as they led each other back inside, and I could see the despair in their bent bodies.

And I understood, Father, unlike those young people on desk, who probably didn't even notice the grief that the old couple was experiencing. They just continued to laugh, kiss and have fun. Yes, I understood. It was funny, Father. I haven't cried in years. I mean, ever since that day on that cold, wind swept pier on Coney Island, when death called, and I did not answer, I have not shed a tear.

Now, I felt the tears coming. I fought them. I fought them hard, Father, with everything I had inside me. And I won! I kept them under control, Father. I kept them under control! I forced myself to break away from that awful scene.

I walked back inside the boat and quietly sat in a corner, and put my head down, and kept it down for the rest of the ride.

***

I must say, as an interesting aside, my trip was somewhat successful, however. I was able to take the slow, quiet Fusion bus to 181st street and Belmont Avenue, to this strange old white guy, who lived in the basement of one of those old tenement buildings that you must have walked by as a young boy.

I fully expected a dark, dank littler place full of junkies and rats, and who knew what else. I was especially worried because I knew I had a pocket full of cash. But dressed as I was, I seriously doubted if anyone would have guessed just how loaded I was.

Walking around with a pocket full of money, looking like death warmed over, was one of my favorite little games! Plus, I still felt that I could hold my own with any dumbbell that was foolish enough to try and attack me!

This old man's basement apartment was extremely neat, and well lit. He had rows and rows of old CD's and video games, and hard to find VHS and DVD movies. But where was the vinyl? Had I already wasted half a day? Had I exposed myself to all kinds of danger and bad memories for nothing?

"Ah, young man, wait, wait. Just a minute," he said, no doubt noticing how disappointed my body language became after he told me that he was all out of vinyl of any kind.

His face brightened up. We walked over to a little locked cabinet. He unlocked it and fished around inside.

"I knew it! I knew it!" he said happily. "I knew I still had them. Just slipped my mind. Look young man, look!"

He held up two round 45's. "Its doo wop, young man. doo wop. You can't find that anywhere."

My heart started pounding. "Yes!" I thought. "Yes!"

As I look back on it, I can see how you would have cracked up watching us. This old guy acted as weird as me. We both talked and negotiated for over an hour over those two 45's, but only occasionally looking at each other. Mostly he spoke with the same weariness I could hear echoing in my own voice.

The Manhattan Syndrome, I suppose. There was certainly a lot of it around. Over 9 million of us from Staten Island, Brooklyn, The Bronx, Queens, could have been in Manhattan that day. And this is not even to mention those squares from Long Island, New Jersey and Connecticut! And what about all of those people from the rest of the country, or the world, for that matter? Those crazy frustrated bastards in Vermont sure knew how to put a hurting on us, Father!

On the way back to Brooklyn with the two old doo wops, I was still somewhat disappointed that they were not the full LP I lad been led to except to find before I made the long trip. But they were doo woo, nevertheless, which was a great find, even through they cost me my entire Army pension check for the month.

Whatever world-weariness and Manhattan Syndrome the old white man suffered from, I still couldn't budge him off of his outrageous price.

"Are you kidding? This ain't that phony black market stuff. This is the original. Here," he said, letting me touch the 45 while he still held on tightly to it. "See. Go head. Feel it." I glanced briefly at his face and saw a real spark, as I had seen when he first remembered that he had this hidden treasure.

I touched the smooth surface, which surprisingly, from what I could see, was thankfully free of scratches. I have paid big dollars in the past and gotten home and could barely hear what was one those records they were so badly worn. But this didn't seem like the case, this time. I knew the old man was right. I could tell that this was the real stuff.

"Two Grand, that's it."

I tried one of my favorite tricks of taking the money out and flashing it before his nose, hoping to provoke a greedy grasping for the hard to find dollars.

This old bastard wasn't biting, Father.

"You shitting me, right!" He still didn't look directly at my money or me.

Still, I liked this old guy for some reason. I loved the tough guy Bronx accent. Those guys used to think that they were as badass as us Brooklynites! Can you believe that, Father!

Oh, sorry, Father. I forgot you were born in the Bronx. No disrespect intended.

But, Father, I wasn't shitting him. Two Grand for two fuckin 45's was enough. I mean, what the fuck did he think I was, a retired General! I was only a Major, for Christ sakes!

But in the end, who cared what they cost. He got his two grand somewhat reluctantly, seeing that I wasn't going to budge.

I loved doo wop more than any other kind of 20th century music. Man, those cats could sing. Their beautiful, clear, passionate, naïve voices made me feel much better about life ("Life is but a dream…ohhhhh weeeeeee.")

Gina loved that shit as well. We used to smoke pot and make love to them all the time.

You were one lucky man, Father, to have lived when you did. The music was great, new, exciting back then. I bet you even saw some of those slick looking guys, with their processed hair; and those gorgeous young babes, in those great looking outfits, prancing all around the stage! What an honor that must have been.

***

On the way back to Brooklyn, I settled down for the long boat ride. I sat down quietly in the same corner of the same boat, eyes down, holding on tightly to my precious find, smiling silently to myself

It was starting to get dark, but even with that, no matter what, I wasn't going to look out the window, or even look up, until we arrive back in Brooklyn. Nothing was going to spoil this rare moment of pure joy, and deep satisfaction.

Chapter 12

Meanwhile, Father, I told you that this letter was going to jump all over the place, but back to the beach in Brighton Beach. This young person was actually talking to me, as if she was some kind of friend. I usually look the other way when people talk to me, like most of us with the Manhattan Syndrome. We just didn't want anyone to get that close to us anymore or invade our private space in any way.

But I looked closely at the young lady. I was sitting on a bench facing the gray ocean, freezing my black Russian ass off! What the fuck I was doing out here in this so-called spring weather is beyond me. But a routine is a routine.

Just like I use to hang out almost every other evening in one of my clubs before the Big Bang, I now sit on a bench in Brighton Beach almost everyday, weather permitting, as part of the routine I have worked out over the years. I sometimes walk the beach, doing my talking to you, Mother, and my old friends. But sometimes my head is totally empty, with only occasional snatches of old songs, which I hum over and over.

It was that rare day of pure emptiness that I most desired.

I have had two other so-called doctors and numerous caregivers since Dr. Anderson gave up on me and moved back to Chicago. Maybe she was right. She told me just before she left that I just didn't want any help. I just wanted to spend the rest of my life wallowing in my grief and lost.

But, this was one of those rare days of pure emptiness. Not a thought of caregivers or doctors. Maybe that's why I was so surprised, even startled by her. Who was this person mentioning Mother's name, and seeming to know who I was? What was this, Father?

The young woman had a youthful, open face. It was hard to tell, but she looked to be in her late twenties. She wore a black knit cap pulled down around her ears, with strands of blond hair escaping from beneath it.

I could see that she wasn't beautiful like Mother. In fact, she was rather plain looking. She had the same small blue eyes, but her lips weren't large, and well-shaped like Mother's. But, she had such a bright, lively, intelligent, happy look on her face. It was a face that showed no fear whatsoever.

Her face also had that oval, Slavic feature which I immediately recognized. I would bet anything she was a full-blooded Russian.

"How do you know who I am?" I asked. I looked at her and quickly looked away.

"I see you all the time. See," she said, turning and pointing to a building on Brightwater directly in back of us. "I live in that building. 301. Haven't you seen me before?"

I quickly looked at her and looked away.

I was unable to place her face. To me everybody looked alike these days, even on the warm days when all those heavy coats came off.

"No, I can't say that I do," I answered.

She didn't seem put off by my answer. "Well I know who you are. My Grandmother told me who you were. I have wanted to come up to you and say hello for a long time. When I look at you when you walk by me, you always look the other way. Grandmother said that I should leave you alone. That you had a lot on your mind. Your mother was soooo very famous, you know. Grandmother starred in that famous version of Uncle Vanya that your mother directed. Grandmother said that all the press came.

"Grandmother has shown me over and over all the pictures of her in the papers with your mother. She said that your mother was a gifted director and actress. That she was the most important actress in Brooklyn. She just should have stayed away from that bad man, who was shot in the street. You should hear my Grandmother talk about your mother. Boy, does she admire that woman!"

My God, Father, this young person just went on, and on, and on, talking to me with such ease, as if we were old, old friends!

I knew she was right about one thing. I knew people saw me over and over again walking the beach. But most of them, thankfully, paid me little mind, except the hookers. I was just one more of those dazed, crazed folks who had survived the Big Bang.

I found myself listening carefully and responding to this young woman. I guess in the back of my mind, this was what I wanted. I guess I really wanted someone to just walk up to me in open friendship, and not be afraid of me, and help pull me out of this shell. This never happened before now, Father. People avoided me, and the shell over the years just hardened.

But here she was, talking away. Talking to me, Father, like I was a trusted old friend. I even smiled openly at how she described Mother.

Now as I write this letter to you, I love the selected memory of older people. That play was so long ago, almost another lifetime. I just had to smile at the thought that Mother was the most "important" actress in all of great big Brooklyn, and was "sooooo famous."

If I remember it correctly, her fame never spread beyond the small world of Russian speaking immigrants

"Do you remember what role she played?" I asked. I was trying to connect the face of this woman, with the faces of the people I vaguely remembered years ago in that small, little theatre as they went through their paces, with Mother ordering them around the stage in Russian, with her sure, insistent voice.

"Yes, she played Helen," the young woman answered.

I thought for a moment. Then I suddenly saw her Grandmother clearly in my mind's eye. Yes, the young Helen. I looked again a little closer at the person sitting on the beach next to me. This had had to be the first time in a long time I have look so closely at anyone in years. Yes, I could see her Grandmother.

I also could see Mother telling her Grandmother in Russian: "You have to feel what this person is feeling. Watch me."

Mother deftly stepped out of the role as the middle-aged stern, wise Mrs. Voynitsky and started taking over the role of the young 27-year-old Helen.

We all watched Mother, transfixed.

"You see, that's how it's played," she said gently to the young woman. "Try it like that."

"I think I remember her," I said to the young woman. I felt a level of enthusiasm rising in me. This was bringing back an unsuspected surge of old, pleasant memories. I quickly pushed the feeling away.

"You do!" she said with delight.

"Yes," I said. "I can see her. I can see her walking across the stage. Yes, I know who she is."

Before she could ask me another question, I asked her one. "Do you still live with your Grandmother?" I didn't know what else to ask her, but for some reason I wanted to continue talking with her.

"Yes, yes. She's old now. All she really wants is to go back to Russia and die." For the first time I saw her face filled with sadness.

"Ah, to die in Russia! What an honor that would be; I think I understand," I said to her softly in Russian, not sure if she understood the language, but really not caring if she did, or not. The words just came from me spontaneously.

She looked at me with total surprise registering on her young face.

"You speak Russian! I speak Russian too. Well I really don't speak Russian, but you know what I mean. Have you been to Russia?" she asked with youthful eagerness.

"No. Mother taught me Russian. That's mostly what we spoke," I said to her in English. "But I wish I had visited mother Russia. How much I wish. America stinks."

I now knew she felt the bitterness in my voice. This is the main reason why I avoided people. I knew that I had in me so much bitterness that I didn't want anyone else to experience what I felt inside.

She nodded her head in agreement. "Things don't look good, that's for sure. We just have to do something about it, don't we? We just can't let those people win, can we?"

It was interesting, Father. It was the subtle change in her demeanor I noticed first. She wasn't asking a question, she was making a statement! That's when I first saw that flash of toughness. Twenty years in the military had taught me to recognize that look, that tone of voice. That was the tone and look of a warrior!

Still, I didn't know what the hell she was talking about. Who were "those people," and who was going to do something about it? But the way she said what she said was so direct, so to the point that I took notice, and became even more interested in her.

Suddenly, she took off her right glove and reached out her hand. "I'm Lucy."

I almost laughed, Father. Only a person so young would do something like that.

I took off my right glove and took her hand and shook it up and down lightly. "Alexander. Alexander Pushkin Litvinova." I gave her my full name because Mother said it was an Old World Russian custom.

"It's good to know you," I said to her in Russian.

Now I was showing off a little, which surprised me. I didn't know I had any show off left in me.

She thought for a moment, still holding on to my hand. I could see she was trying to find the right words in Russian.

Finally, she started pumping my hand up and down again, smiling widely, displaying small teeth much like Mother's, and saying in broken Russian "Know you is good to know."

Father, I know that you can fully appreciate this rare moment of history repeating itself and smile a little smile of recognition. All at once this Lucy person reminded me of Mother. Mother could never quite get her English right. You captured it perfectly in your famous short story, "The Queen of Macy's."

Now it was Lucy who couldn't get her Russian right! But it didn't matter, just as it must have not mattered to you, Father. You knew what Mother meant, just as I now knew what Lucy meant, although it didn't quite come out the way it should have.

We both put our gloves back on. I didn't laugh, or smile at Lucy's mistake, although it was clear that she didn't speak much Russian.

"You know what? You should come over and meet my Grandmother. You are one of the few people around here who can still speak Russian." Her voice was filled with excitement and decisiveness.

"Come over to your place?" I asked. I could feel my voice shake slightly. I know now how my voice must have sounded, Father. This person was inviting me over to her apartment. Me, the mad black Russian who walked Brighton Beach, often unshaven, withdrawn, spooky looking, ghost-like, often talking aloud to unseen sprits long since passed.

"Oh, come on! I know you live nearby," she said, clearly not willing to take no for an answer. "I want you to meet Grandmother. And," she said, phasing. "I want you to teach me Russian."

“Me? Teach you Russian? Are you serious?”

“Yeah, yeah,” she answered excitedly, jumping up and down on the park bench like a young teenager. “Can you write in Russian?”

“A little. Not much.”

“Oh, that’s ok. All I want to do is learn to speak it. Oh, this is going to be soooo exciting. It is a date, Alexander?”

“Ah, you can call me Alex.”

“No,” she said. “I like Alexander better. It has force to it. It’s a great name. So, is it a date, Alexander?”

Once again, Father, she was decisive and to the point.

Chapter 13

You should see me, Father! I can't believe it. But it's true, Father. So true.

I'm standing in front of my bathroom mirror, shaving and preparing myself for dinner with Lucy Libid, and her grandmother, Anna K. Libid. And, I was taking inventory on myself.

I was 53 years old. But, I still had my health and my well-built, 6'3 body. My teeth were still intact, still white and even. Mother's bright blue eyes shown clearly from my light tan, cooper face. If I might say so, I'm still handsome in a rugged, aging kind of way. I kept my head shaven so I didn't know if I had any real hair left or not.

Maybe, Father, all those years of military training had imprinted me permanently, because I still got up each morning and did my push-ups. I still cooked and ate the right food. My body was in great shape; it was just my mind that's all fucked up.

Lucy had made sure that I was going to make this date by setting the time, the place and date right there on the bench! She pulled out a small, wooden pencil and little card and wrote down her address and e-number.

She pushed the note with the information into my hands, and the look on her face said I better not, not show up. It was a good thing that she went to all this effort, because if she had been causal about it, I know I would have found a reason not to go.

***

As soon as I got back to my apartment, I hurriedly looked through box after box, and opened and closed drawers, until I found the well-preserved program for Uncle Vanya, with a picture of the cast.

I knew it was here! The moment I remembered who her grandmother was, my mind quickly flashed on that program. As I looked at it, I smiled to myself. I was so glad to have found it.

I remembered witnessing a little fight between Mother and The Gangster over that program. Mother, as always, wanted only the best, which meant glossy paper, coated stock, with a full color photo of the cast members on the back page, to top it off.

The Gangster was beside himself! He was huffing and puffing all around our living room. He just didn't want to spend that kind of money on a fancy program.

"No, Shasa! No, damnit!" he shouted loudly at her in English. "Better to spend the money on an ad. Why spend that kind of money for just a program?"

For a brief moment, Father, I thought that I heard for the first time, the mean, ruthless, brutal Gangster in his voice. The same Gangster people lowered their voices and eyes, and softly whispered about whenever he past them on the crowded streets of Brighton Beach.

But how wrong I was, Father.

"Just a program?" Mother answered back in a cool, no nonsense voice in her precise Russian. She put her hands on her thin hips and fixed her small, cold blue eyes on him, now even smaller than usual.

"Ok! Ok!" The Gangster said quickly, throwing up his hands in defeat, the hardness all but gone from his voice.

Talk about a weenie, Father!

It obviously didn't take much for Mother to get her way with this man! I only smiled to myself at what a pushover he was. It was hard to believe that he was a hard-ass Gangster, the way Mother was always pushing him around, grabbing him by his ankles and shaking every dine out of him, whenever she wanted.

It was a good thing that Mother was so persistent (and spoiled rotten, I might add!). As I looked at the program, that photo of them looked as if it was taken yesterday. There was Mother in a big white wig, looking all the world like an Old-World Russian. And there was the pretty young Anna K. Libid.

If my calculations are correct, Lucy's grandmother must be at least 67 or 68 years old, given that I was only fifteen when we first met so many years ago. When she played the young Helen, she could have been the same age as Lucy is now.

I remembered Mother complaining about now hard it was to fill that key part because so few young actresses spoke Russian.

"All they want do is work in Manhattan. Manhattan this! Manhattan that!" She said at one dinner. Mother spoke with growing frustration, wringing her hands in despair, then dramatically throwing them up to the high heavens.

I didn't know what to say to her, so I kept my head down and concentrated on my food.

I can still see the happy look on Mother's face just a few nights later as she couldn't wait to tell me the good news.

Dinner was already waiting for me as I returned home, late, after hanging out with the guys longer than I should have. I had spent the afternoon at the nearby New York Aquarium. I never get enough of the place. I'm always deeply entranced by all the life floating endlessly around and around.

I was worried as I hurried home. We had dinner together almost always at the same time. I am convinced that this is why we bonded so closely, Father. She didn't behave like my friends' mothers. I couldn't take my food in my room and sit and watch something while I ate. We both sat down together each night, at almost exactly the same time, whether she had to go to the theatre, go to work, or whatever.

Mother had to budget her time, which she became an expert at. That's why she was always slightly pissed off if I came in late.

But not this night, Father! Mother wasn't interested in any whys I might have for being late. To my relief, she was not angry at all. Her face filled with happiness as I walked in the door. She was just so glad to see me.

"She just walked in!" she said excitedly as we sat down for dinner. "What the hell was I supposed to do, Alex, close the damn play down? But she just walked in. I didn't even know she was coming. She said someone just told her I needed an actress. Can you believe that, Alex!

"I could see Helen."

Mother held up her hand and made a small spyglass. "That's Helen! I say. I hope this bitch knows now to act, I say. Then she read. How she read.

"She good, Alex," Mother said confidently. "Speaks perfect Russian."

I looked up from my delicious soup and smiled at her, as pleased as she obviously was.

Mother was so excited as she cursed joyfully in both Russian and English, telling me this good news. This time, however, she didn't wring her thin, white hands, but kept blowing the high heavens big kisses.

I loved that woman, Father! Especially at moments like this. She could be so dramatic!

It seemed that Anna Libid had only been in the US for a few years, and her English was only a shade worse than Mother's. But Mother said that she was very educated and spoke the kind of Russian the great Chekhov demanded.

As I looked at all those wonderful artists on that old program, led by Mother, it all started slowly coming back. I started feeling a level of good feeling rising in me. I can't remember the last time I felt like this.

I also got that funny feeling I had the day of the Big Bang. That some how, some way, nosy Mother was once again quietly intervening in my life; subtlety, but surely helping me avoid a major catastrophe.

How else to explain this, Father?

***

I know you have no doubt been quietly wondering what I have done for a love life during this long period. One thing I know clearly about you, which literally dripped from the pages of your novels, was that you thought sex between men and women was the greatest gift God gave human beings.

I mean, after all, you are the author of the infamous novel, *The Woman's Man.*

Wow! What a read that novel was, Father, with sperm flying all over the place! Tsk! Tsk! my man, as you guys might say. But as pumped as you were about sex and romance, I'm sad to report that your only son has been anything but a woman's man since the Big Bang.

Hoes, as you guys called them—prostitutes, hookers, streetwalkers, whatever they are called, have been enough for me. Speaking of hookers, Father, they are everywhere. You can't walk the boardwalk without someone trying to pick you up.

That's one of the reasons why I was so suspicious when Lucy first spoke to me. Was she a hooker? Or even worse, was she one of those goddamn caregivers?

All of those reverends in Washington tried to cleanse our souls, and now our streets are filled with women, young and old, selling themselves to any man willing to pay. What was better, Father, women in the workplace, or the armed forces, or the streets?

You won't find many young men on the streets. Sure, if you look hard enough you can find them as well. I have seen them hiding in the shadows, beckoning me. But they knew, and I knew, what would happen to them if they were caught by The People's Moral Force, with their silly looking, piss-ass uniforms.

Listen to this, Father: they have pointed hats, with little feathers sticking out of the back. I can see you now, rolling around on the floor in laughter. A fucking little feather! Who else but a lame-ass preacher who thinks that he is Neapolitan could approve something like that.

The asshole that designed those damn punk-ass uniforms should have been shot! But if one of those evil bastards ever caught some guy wanting to raise his dirty little butt in your face, then they could be a mean and brutal as we in the mighty army used to be, bad uniforms and all!

But ho's. There were plenty of them. I would walk at night perhaps once or twice a month and just stand in the dark under the Boardwalk and let an eager mouth relieve me of whatever tension had built up.

I never touched them, or grabbed them tightly when I came. I just paid out the money, unzipped my pants, and did what I did, zipped back up, and was gone.

That was my love life, Father.

Chapter 14

I was nervous, to say the least, Father, as I rang the downstairs bell at Lucy's old tenement. Most of the old buildings had been torn down, replaced by huge high-rises. Mother became very angry when they started building those big buildings.

"Big and ugly, Alex."

This building had seen better days, but it was still standing in a choice spot overlooking the ocean. There were so many unanswered questions: did Lucy live here with her grandmother? Or, was she just one of those professional caregivers assigned to keep an eye on us Manhattan Syndrome types?

I guess you can tell by now, Father, I hated those bastards with a passion. They always seemed to show up when you don't want to see them, which is never! First the witch doctors, then them! All part of the same industry set up to so-called help us, but really to give a lot of money and control over people's lives to a bunch of highly selected people: our President for Life, Reverend Guess's new effete elite.

But, what was I to expect? Maybe this was just one of those old-fashioned, multi-generational immigrant families with brothers, uncles, sisters, fathers and mothers? And, what could Lucy want from me, except Russian lessons?

"Yes?"

"Alexander."

Lucy buzzed me up, and soon I found myself being introduced to a round, jolly-looking, fat old lady.

"Grandmother, this is Alexander."

The woman struggled mightily to get up from her chair.

"No. No," I said, motioning for her to stay put. "Stay seated."

She thankfully settled back down.

"Hello Alex," she said. "It's been a long time since we last spoke. Your mother and I were such good friends. Sit down, young man. Have a seat. Lucy, ask Alex if he wants something to drink. A little vodka, perhaps?"

As to be expected, the apartment was dimly lit. These days you could not buy a light bulb over 35 watts, and caregivers would poke around your apartment to make sure that there was only one lamp per room.

Anna Libid spoke rapidly, with only a touch of a Russian accent. It was hard to believe that this was the same person I met at the Pushkin

Playhouse so many years ago, but she didn't look or sound like someone who was looking for a place to go and die.

Her voice was buoyant, confident, playful even. I also noticed through the dim light that she was heavily made up, and her hair was all puffed up in a giant gray bouffant. She looked as if she had just walked out of the hairdresser's.

To top off her great looking do, she had on a long, fancy blue dress, a gold speckled blue and gray shawl, and a long string of pearls. She looked outrageous, Father!

I couldn't imagine anyone sitting around her dim apartment, dressed like that on a regular basis. This clearly must be a special evening for her.

Lucy laughed easily at her grandmother's enthusiastic behavior.

"Grandmother, at least let Alexander take off his coat before you start ordering us about."

Anna Libid rolled her large, gray eyes upward dramatically, in one of Mother's grand theatrical gestures, and threw her hands in the air. These old actresses are all the same, Father!

"What's an old lady to do, Alex? She's always picking on me!"

For some reason, I was enjoying all this lighthearted banter. Just as Lucy had put me at ease the other day on the beach, her grandmother had done the same thing in a manner of minutes.

I handed Lucy my coat and gloves. When I tried to push my black watch cap into my coat pocket, I felt the old program. I had brought it along as a conversation starter, because I was unsure how I would handle myself or if I would have anything to say.

I pulled it out. "Look," I said, handing it to her, and saying in Russian, "I brought you a little present."

I watched as her gray eyes lit up with delight, both by my Russian and my little present. I had guessed right! I hoped that she hadn't seen this program in years.

"Oh, Alex!" she said.

She gently took the program from my hand, almost as if she were afraid to damage it. She held it lovingly to her chest, in a warm embrace.

You won't believe this, Father, but this fat old lady sprang up from her chair and gave me a big bear hug..

"Madame Litvinova always said you were a good boy," she whispered in my ear in Russian. I could smell layers of perfume and powder, and who knows what else she had applied to that overly made-up face of hers..

I briefly glanced over at Lucy. She seemed pleased. She was smiling like crazy. I knew she could sense that I was relaxed and had been completely won over by her grandmother. Her instincts on that cold bench had proven to be correct..

I sat down on the small couch next to Anna, trying to decide if I should really chance some vodka. All real Russians drank vodka. I knew that. But, I was afraid of the stuff, Father..

No matter what demons haunted me in the interiors of my mind, I still had not given myself to alcoholic despair, as so many of us with the Manhattan Syndrome had done. That wine I drank every evening when I could make a score was good stuff, not cheap shit. Being a ranking Officer in the U.S. Military was more about kicking ass. We were also gentlemen, Father..

Finding good wine could be a bitch, but it was worth it, and it didn't pack the wallop that the same amount of vodka, gin, or Colonel Bird's good, old bourbon would have packed..

But why not a little taste of vodka tonight? So far, this had turned into a most promising evening, the most promising evening I had experience in a long time..

Lucy went into the kitchen to fix us vodkas on the rocks.

As soon as she left, Anna K. Libid leaned over to me and said in Russian, her face not so jolly now, "You've had a rough time, haven't you, Alex?".

I lowered my head and felt the sadness returning.

"Don't feel so bad," she said, sensing that she'd touched the wrong button. "Lucy has also suffered. And so, have I. She's like you, Alex, only half-Russian, poor child. Her mother was Irish, or American Irish, or something like that. Who knows with you Americans, what you are?"   .

I looked at her more closely. I hadn't noticed the Manhattan Syndrome on either her or Lucy.

"How has she suffered?" I asked in Russian.

"Her mother and father were both killed that day. And, all her mother's family. I also lost my only son, my only child. You know, we Russian don't have many kids like you Americans do. I was all she had left. I had to take her in."

Anna spoke rapidly in Russian with a lowered voice, as if she didn't want anyone else to hear what we were talking about, as if only I needed to have this important bit of information so I could better understand her granddaughter.

Lucy returned, interrupting us. She handed us our drinks and settled down in a chair right across from me. I didn't know if she now sensed that I now knew something about her that I hadn't known when she left the room for our drinks..

But, it was funny, Father. I was glad to hear what I heard. I now knew that I could trust her. She wasn't a phony caregiver, making a living off the misery of others and spying on us for the Clerics. Lucy was a real person! That news shifted the gloom I had experienced from Anna's questions and made me feel hopeful again..

"Look, child." Anna reached over and handed Lucy the prized program with her chubby hand.

"Which is Mrs. Litvinova, the one with the white hair?" Lucy asked. She directed her question to me. She looked closely at the photo of the cast on the back of the program, holding it up the dim light..

"Yes, that's Mother."

"And, look at you, grandmother! You were soooo beautiful."

Father, you should have seen the look of pride on Anna K. Libid's face. I thought that she was about to burst. "It was such a wonderful play. Your mother was so good. What a director!"

"And, she was a good actress," I added.

"A good actress?" Mrs. Libid asked. She looked at me with disbelieving, intimidating eyes..

Against my will, I started moving around uneasily in my chair. How could I have had the nerve to say such a thing in her presence!

"What do you mean a good actress?" Anna Libid said forcefully. "She was the best!".

Anna waved a fat hand at me, dismissing my foolishness.

"Ah, it was the play of a lifetime," she went on, cooling down from my transgression. "Like no other I have done. There's never been anything like it." I could see that Anna was back in a pleasant world of her own

Mother's world. A comfortable world of similar types. A lovely world. A world of heavy make-up, false mustaches, oversized wigs, fake laughter, long, grand speeches, tears, joy, much applause, lingering bows—the best of all possible worlds. The magic world of imagination and make believe.

Anna spoke in a dramatic fashion, as if every word had deep meaning and profound significance, as if she was back on the small stage of the Pushkin Playhouse, with Mother looking on. This was Anna's evening. I clearly had invoked something in her, and Mrs. Libid held court, almost as if Lucy and I were not even in the room. Only once did she fully direct her conversation toward me.

"I was at your mother's funeral. God rest her soul! That's when I saw you in that fabulous looking uniform! You were so tall and handsome, with all those ribbons. You should have seen him Lucy. He could have made you faint. I just looked at you and felt so sorry for you. I wanted to come over and give you a big hug. What you had with your mother was real special. All she did was talk about you. Alex, this! Alex, that! She loved you so much." I could see out of the corner of my eye that Lucy was becoming interested in what her grandmother was saying. She was lighting candles as we had used our share of electricity for the evening. She stopped what she was doing and stared at me.

"What were you, a sergeant?" she asked.

"Don't be silly, child," Anna answered quickly, stopping me before I had a chance to say anything. "He was a big-time officer in the United States

Army. A Colonel. Or was it a General? You should have seen all the ribbons, child.

"I laughed softly. I remembered the service, with Mother lying silently, peacefully in her coffin, as the strange-looking priests said words over her. I had showed up in full military dress, in honor of Mother.

Notwithstanding you, and no disrespect intended, Father, but I think my love for the military is in my Russian genes. Military officers were always a big deal in Russia. Mother's family, as you probably know, came from a long line of high-ranking military officers, or that's what she told me.

Whatever the case, Mother was so proud of me and loved it when I wore my uniform. She would walk down Brighton Beach Avenue, making her way through the bustling throngs and holding on tightly to my arm, with this pleased look on her face. I knew what that look said, Father. I had just made Major before she died and was now entitled to wear the gold braids on my hat. Anna K. Libid was correct. I cut quite a dashing figure!

Still, I wasn't no damn Colonel, Father, much less a General!

"Your grandmother is more than generous," I said to Lucy. "I was only a Major."

"You know, that reminds me of a play I did on Broadway. I loved Broadway, before those idiots ruined everything! You should have seen Broadway, Lucy, in those days. It was so glamorous. So very glamorous."Anna Libid continued her endless patter, reliving play after play. She talked and talked. I kept looking at Lucy, and she kept looking at me and pushing more vodka my way. Suddenly, at long last, Anna yawned mightily.

"Oh, I'm so tired," she said to me in Russian.

"We must get our rest. Rest makes you strong," I said back to her in Russian.She slowly pulled herself up from the chair. "You stay, Alex. Keep Lucy company. And, you come back, you hear me! We are family."She quickly disappeared into an inner room, taking her powder and perfume with her.But what a great old lady she turned out to be, Father.

"Would you like another drink" Lucy asked as soon as her grandmother left.I thought for a second. My head was already woozy. I could tell that I was very close to that moment when just a little more booze would push me over the edge into drunkenness. "No. I think I will just finish this."

All at once an awkward silence settled between us. I stared down at what was left of my watered-down drink and took a small sip. I wanted to extend the life of this drink as long as I could.

"You know, your grandmother told me about what happened to your parents.

"Lucy's face filled with annoyance. "She did! That old bitch. When did she tell you that! I bet she even told you I am only half-Russian. That I am really Irish. I'm as Russian as she is. Sometimes I could really kill that woman.

"I could hear the anger in her voice. I was amazed at how quickly she could go from pleasant to angry.

"I'm sorry," I said. "I shouldn't have brought it up. Look, I've got to go".

"I still think I should go."

I wanted to get away from her because I no longer had Anna as a buffer. What could I say to her. Also, I wanted to kiss her. It was the strangest thing, Father. I hadn't kissed a woman since Gina, and you know how long ago that was! I wanted to press my lips to her little, heart-shaped lips and pull her close to me. As Lucy talked, I heard little of what she was saying because I was looking so hard at her exciting lips.She got my coat and gloves and we stood by her door.

"When do we start our lesson, Alexander?"

"Aaah, I don't know. When?"

"How about tomorrow?"

"Tomorrow?"

"Yes. Why not? Grandmother goes to the senior center for lunch and to gab with her girlfriends. Also, as old as she is, there's some old guy there she's trying to fuck. So, come over at one."The word "fuck," and the bold way she said it, sent a small shock wave through me."Are you sure?"

"Of course, I'm sure. Why shouldn't I be sure?"

The awkward silence between us returned. But, Lucy, as always, made the first move. "Let me give you a hug, Alexander.

"She put her arms around me and hugged me tight. Not the friendly, motherly bear hug that her grandmother had given me, but a passionate, sexual, loving hug.

I put my arms around her. I was so much taller and bigger than she, and she just seemed to melt and disappear in my arms. I felt an overwhelming emotion swelling up in me. Through my heavy overcoat, her body heat was rising, gauge after gauge.

I bent down and kissed her, the way I had wanted to kiss her all night. She returned my kiss with real passion. Tears started running down her face. I hugged her even closer, and Father, tears started running down my face too.

Yes, real live tears, the first tears I had shed since that evening on the Coney Island pier. Both of us shook with emotion, as years of pent-up feelings poured into each other.

It was incredible, Father.

As I walked the short blocks back to 3099, I felt as if a 50-story building had been lifted from my back. Normally, I would have walked the darkest, quietest street, which would have been Brightwater. Instead, this night I decided to walk up to Brighton Beach Avenue.

I was not used to being out so late, although it couldn't have been more than ten o'clock. In the old days, I would be just getting ready to go out. I noticed things I never noticed before. Despite the freezing night, the avenue was packed with people. The old El creaked nosily overhead. People were still out shopping at the stores; some that still had old signs in Russian. I saw young couples, so full of life, so unconcerned with Clerics and caregivers. I even spotted a pair of those asshole Moral Force guys with those fuck-up-looking hats. I saw several old ladies walking trancelike, unconcerned by others, as unconcerned by others as I once was. I heard loud laughter from a bar on the corner. A young hooker stared me dead in the face and winked at me. I smiled back at the young black woman, who couldn't have been more than fifteen years old.

As I turned onto my block, I looked up at the dim-lit apartment windows. I saw the shadows of people going about their daily lives, moving from room to room. It was life that I saw, Father. Life!

Maybe that's all I needed to do, after these years of seeing witch doctors and caregivers and listening to bullshit? Maybe all I needed was a big, warm hug, a passionate kiss, and a good cry to make life reappear?

Isn't that something, Father?

Chapter 15

I can see you now, Father, dabbing your old, dark eyes, and saying,

"good form, son! Well done, boy! You snapped out of it just in time, and

allowed your ever-watching mother to once again guide you down the right

path.

"And now you have your beautiful Russian bride, in the same way I

found my beloved Shasa."

But, please, Father, before you start getting carried away and start

giving me high-fives or one of those other corny things you guys used to do

in your century, there is a lot more to this story. A whole lot more. Lucy and

I just didn't ride off happily into the sunset like in one of those old movies

from your century.

One thing is true, Lucy and I rarely spent a day not seeing each other

from that first evening on. We had touched each other in a real way, and

Lucy was not about to let me go; and, Father, I didn't want to be let go.

I learned over our so-called Russian lessons that both she and Anna K

Libid collected disability from the Manhattan Syndrome Fund, although,

except for that crying spell at our first kiss, I still could not detect in either

one of them even an appearance of that strange numbness of the spirit.

Maybe it was because Anna had only been in this country for so little time or because Lucy was so young, but neither of them seemed to have fully absorbed the enormity of what had happened. It was more than just the loss of a mother or a son or a father, although those were bad enough.

Each month they both received their little check from the Federal government, and Anna, because of her age, did not have to go see a witch doctor and only had to put up with the unpredictable visits from the caregivers.

The cynic inside of me said that they were getting those checks not because of any "syndrome" but because they were Russian. When I was growing up, both in Los Angeles and New York, that was always the rap on the Russians: no matter what the government program, they would find a way to get the most out of it. Their critics said it was a holdover from Communism.

This negative image of Russians as being opportunist lay-abouts so pissed off Mother that even when she could have asked for help, being a single mother and all, she refused.

"Who needs that. Let them keep it." She once said with a haughty toss of her head. She had practically slammed the door in the face of a social worker that came to our door and told her that she could get food stamps.

Mother could afford to be contemptuous in those days, because she had her job at the bookstore, your little gifts of intellectual property, and, of course, the more than generous gifts from the ever-gracious gangster.

It soon became clear after only a few days of going to her apartment that Lucy wasn't all of that interested in learning Russian. What she *was* interested in was my Army background and me.

"Did you fly when you were in the Army. I mean in a real airplane?" she asked eagerly on the second day, out of nowhere.

"Of course, how else could we get to where we were going? They were sending us all over the damn world."

A wistful look came over her face. "What was it like? What was it like being so far up in the air? They won't let us fly anymore. I just wish for once I could sit in an airplane and ride around in the clouds."

Before I could say anything, she asked another question.

"Did you ever kill anybody? Were those ribbons grandmother mentioned because you killed a lot of people?"

I laughed. "Let's put it like this. You see a cluster of personnel in the distance. You tell your loader and gunner to load an anti-personnel round. Then you blast the shit out of them. Did you kill them? Who knows?"

"Their dumb asses just ain't around no more!" she said quickly. Lucy started laughing like crazy. I was really starting to like this woman, Father. I already told you how we vets like telling war stories.

"Tell me, did you ever get shot?"

"Damn right I was shot! Want to see the wounds?" I impulsively unbuttoned my shirt and showed her the scars from my wounds.

"Wow!" Her eyes widened as she reached over and gently touched my shoulder. "Wow!"

On the third day, she asked me a highly unusual question.

"Do you believe in the Manhattan Syndrome?"

Hummm. What could I say? I know that I saw all those crazed looking zombies walking all over the place. I was once one of them, just days ago, and still was in many ways. I still felt the pain and sense of absence. If it wasn't the Manhattan Syndrome, then what was it? It was some kind of syndrome. Who cared what they called it?

"Sure. It's just a name," I said.

"But a name for what" Lucy answered back angrily. Once again, I saw that quick switch in her personality. "For thought control? So that the government could have an excuse to tell us what to do in whatever we wanted to do. Now we have to prove that we go to church at least once a month or we could be removed from the rolls."

"You're kidding?"

Lucy looked at me with a look of disbelief, as if to say "what kind of cave you been living in?"

"You're a vet, Alexander. They ain't going to fuck with you, but they sure like fucking with us. By the way, tell me, Major, how do you say fucking in Russian?"

Now her anger was replaced with a little gleam in her eyes as she asked me this deliberately provocative question. I must say, she was certainly an interesting little bitch! I hadn't even tried to fuck her yet. In the good old days, if I wasn't in bed with a woman on the third date, FORGETABOUTIT!

But that was then in a world long gone. This was now. The opening was clear, Father, but I decided not to take it. Not yet. I really liked her and her strange self. I loved those flashes of fire. It reminded me to the people I served with in the military. Bad-asses. My kind of people.

I wanted her to stay with me. I was afraid if I reached over and grabbed her, as I would have done in the past, that I would have guess wrong, and she would throw me out, and never want to see me again.

I couldn't take that chance.

As she walked me to the door, after our "lesson" I was slowly putting my hat and coat on, lingering deliberately, hoping for another kiss at the door, or at least a big hug like I got the day before. I stood there waiting for something to happen but not making any kind of move toward her.

She looked up at me with a bold, teasing smile. She unbuttoned my coat and put her arms around me, pressing her body hard against mine.

"It looks like I'm going to have to do all the work in this relationship," she said in almost a hissing sound. She reached down and put her hands on my crotch, and started rubbing my now hard prick.

"You never did tell me how to say fucking in Russian, Major," she whispered to me.

I unzipped my pants, and she reached in and pulled my penis out. She silently fell to her knees and took it in her warm mouth. She started sucking me off with great skill. I starred rubbing her hair, the first time I had touched a woman while having sex since Gina. My entire body shook as I found myself coming in just a few minutes.

She stood up and kissed me hard, with my sperm all over her face.

"Next time, Major, you're gonna fuck me for real," she said, her little body now ablaze with real heat.

Chapter 16

And fuck her I did! Father. From that point on, the moment I entered the apartment and took my coat off, we were soon laying in her warm bed, sometime fucking, but most of the time just holding on to each other and enjoying the warmth of our bodies against each other.

She was in so much need. I was really surprised, Father, really surprised.

In the next few weeks she revealed even more about herself. She also gave me a modern history and civic lesson. The more she talked, the more I could see that this woman was deadly serious, and carried a deep anger about the conditions and government we lived under.

One day she had just come back from a meeting with her doctor who told her that she was too nervous. "Look at this Alexander."

She held out her hand. There was a bunch of little blue pills in it. "Now they said I should take these. I'm supposed to be too nervous. Who the fuck wouldn't be nervous the way they try to control you. Bullshit! I ain't taking this shit!"

She threw the pills on the floor and started stomping on them in a fit of rage. I had never seen her like this.

"I'm telling you, Alexander, all they want to do is control us. That's all! Well, they ain't gonna control me! Fuck them! Fuck them! Fuck them!"

Lucy was so angry that I didn't know what to say to her.

"Why don't you get a job. That way you don't have to deal with them," I said, trying to sound as reasonable as I could.

She gave me that look again that said I was out of my mind, or at least a bit daffy. "There are no jobs, Alexander! Ever since they dismantled all the plants, and outlawed cars, what is left for us to do? We all can't be farmers. All this talk about everyone getting a little patch of land. What a joke. They just want to get us in the middle of nowhere so they can keep a better eye on us. Who wants to live in the middle of nowhere? Tell me, who the hell cares if there are more trees now. And, fuck deers. Who the fuck wants to be around a bunch of fucking deer's! They say we are all going to die of cancer, except for really black people, unless we do as we're told. I think they're all full of shit."

It's amazing, Father, how little I had noticed of the world around me. I did watch as the cars slowly disappeared, replaced by slow, silent electric personal scooters. Some guy back at the end of your century said that his invention would one day replace cars. You know what, Father, he was right. The Moral Force mainly owns those little things and other bigwigs. Most people walk, bike, or take the subway or Fusion bus.

I could afford it, but I didn't own a personal scooter. What for? I didn't go anywhere, except once in a while on a vinyl or red wine hunt.

All of this was supposed to make the weather better. But, old country Colonel Bird would say that that was like closing the barn door after the horse had already run off.

But, I suppose the weather was getting better, whatever better meant. And talk of the economy, and jobs? I knew nothing, Father.

But it was clear that a person like Lucy was paying attention. And the more I listened to her, the more I could see that she was suffering. Her real Manhattan Syndrome was wondering what was going to happen to her and her feeling that she had little control over her life, as those fools in Washington made bad law after bad law.

What a contrast to me, Father! All I cared about was my vinyl and where I was going to score my next bottle of good wine.

"So, what are you going to do?"

"It's not about what I'm going to do. It's about what we're going to do."

"Who is we?" I asked, confused.

"Those of us who are no longer going to sit still and do nothing."

I watched as her face became tense and steely with determination. Her blue eyes became as cold as Mother's did when she was pissed off at me, or The Gangster.

"I still don't know what you are talking about," I said, unable to say anything else.

She smiled as she noticed the look on my face and came over and put her arms around me and pulled me close to her.

"Major Pushkin, it's time for you to come back into the real world."

***

Her "real world," as it turned out, was a meeting of her friends that she finally convinced me to attend.

We entered into the basement of a house at the end of the block on a street near my apartment. What I found interesting was this block was one of the few left that had the old fashion attached, single-family houses that were so much a part of Brighton Beach when I first moved here. They, like the tenements, have been mostly torn down to make way for the huge high-rises.

The basement was already filled with young people. I quickly looked around and saw that no one looked older than thirty. I felt everyone's eyes fixed on me. I had a spooky feeling. I guess it was just because I wasn't used to being around so many people. I felt that they were all looking at me as if I was guilty of something.

There must have been at least twenty of them. They were all white and Asian, with the notable exception of a very dark-skinned black man with wild looking dreadlocks.

"So, who's your friend?" The person who spoke up was a small, narrowed-eyed Asian man.

"This is Major Litvinova," Lucy said in a loud, formal voice. "I brought him here to meet with us. The Major is a man of action and military training and is as much a victim of this oppression as any of us. And, with his training, he can help us."

"We don't need no damn Major. It's those kinds of motherfuckers that started all of this shit in the first place," the young man answered. He stared at me with dark, accusing eyes.

"That's right! That's right," several people shouted.

I felt like turning around and leaving. I didn't need them, either. Fuck them, whoever they were!

"Goddamnit, Gary, who the hell are you to tell me who I can bring! Now you shut the fuck up. The Major is with me. Now, does anybody else have anything to say about it?"

Whoaaaa, Father. What was going on here? The people in the room, especially the wiseass that had spoken out again me, now looked chastened, put in their place. Lucy seemed in her element. There was not a trace of hesitation or fear in her voice or her body language.

"Look, Commander, we just never can be more careful. We don't know who this is. But if you say he's okay, he's okay," Gary said, making his peace wlth Lucy.

But, what was this "Commander" stuff. A sense of suspicion came over me. Was this what it was all about? Had she set me up from the first day we met on that bench? Was it just because she needed me to help in some little game she was playing with these people?

Chapter 17

As paranoid as those first couple of meetings made me, it was those nights of sleeping with Lucy that convinced me that she needed me for more than just military advice. She clung to me so tightly, wrapping her little body all around me, as if she was afraid I was going to get up and leave.

I would lay quietly awake and stoke her head softly, not wanting to fall asleep, but wanting to continue to feel her warm body next to me. And her small body would often start shaking, and I could feel the warm tears through the darkness.

"What's wrong, Lucy?" I once asked.

"Don't ever leave me, Alexander," she said in a quiet, low voice. She squeezed me tighter than ever before.

I said nothing. I just continued to gently stroke her head, to experience her. I pulled her even tighter in my arms. It seemed as if both of us were trying hard to sink our very selves into each other. I was thinking, why I would ever want to leave her? I was thinking that this is how humans survived all the wars, and big bombs, and bad weather, and scary nights, and diseases, and liars who claimed to know what God wanted from us, and the crazy, the power-hungry, the greedy.

I was just thinking, Father, why would I ever want to leave her? It all boiled down to a dark, quiet night, with two scared people clinging tightly to each other. Like I said to you before, I wasn't no damn intellectual, but I did know that.

"You promise me. You promise."

"Yes, Lucy, I promise."

Needless to say, Father, I became very involved in "Commander" Lucy's underground organization, but from a distance. It was clear that they were dedicated revolutionaries, and Lucy was one of leaders of the Brooklyn cell. They had one goal: to overthrow the government, pure and simple. Even though I was benefiting from the system because of my steady checks, I felt one with these young people.

What they needed from me was not some crazy bomb thrower, but a planner. I mean, what a bunch of jive-ass, half-stepping amateurs. They meant well all right, but the way they were going, all of them were either going to end up dead or in jail. And the last thing I wanted was for Lucy to end up dead, or in jail.

One thing I did know about the Clerics was that these guys were not some mealy-mouth sissies. They had returned to hanging years ago. Lucy said it was because hanging was an energy saver. They had also taken away all the guns, totally outlawing them. Lucy told me that you could get 20 to life for even being in possession of one, with no such thing as an appeal. Even the People's Moral Force was not allowed to carry guns, just big clubs. Only a select group of plainclothes enforcers carried guns.   So, how were these would-be revolutionaries going to overthrow the Clerics and restore democracy to America, when they didn't know the first thing about military planning and had zero fire power. Over many years, I learned many, have tried the old Gandhi method of passive resistance and non-violence. But President for Life Rev. Guess would have none of it.

Now, some wanted to do something even as dramatic as what happened on Oct, 3rd. But I could see that that was just talk. I could see that these folks couldn't build a conventional bomb, much less *the* Bomb.

Others wanted to randomly stab people suspected of being caregivers. That asshole that first gave me a hard time was especially forceful in advocating this kind of action

I didn't say anything at meetings. I just sat silently and listened, my head down, wondering why I was there and wishing that the meeting would end, as Lucy and her friends argued passionately over tactics.

More than once I wanted to get up and leave, to go back to Mother's cozy, familiar apartment and have a bottle of good red wine, and spend my allotted three hours of electricity, quietly listening to my vinyl.

But I remembered my nights in that big bed with Lucy and remembered her warm tears, her great need, my promise never to leave her, her hot body. And the need I felt to be near her, to never leave her, overwhelmed my desire to betray her by just getting up and walking out of the meeting. So, I stayed and listened.

But enough was enough! After my fifth meeting, I told Lucy that I didn't want to attend any more meetings. The five meetings I had attended did, however, create a plan of action in my head. Ideas were slowly forming in my head. I was thinking about things I had not thought about in years. This was the first real systematic thinking I had done in who know how long.

"Lucy, they listen to you. They respect you. You're their leader. I can see that. I can give you advice."

I saw a funny look coming over her face.

"You don't have to agree with anything I say. We can just talk. And you can take what you need and go back and tell them what they need to do.

They don't have to know it's coming from me. Does that make sense to you?"

She thought for a moment, cocking her head to one side in a thoughtful pose. I could guess that she knew in the back of her mind that I was still uncomfortable around people. I don't know if I will ever get my old confidence back and once again experience the joy of being the center of attention in a large crowd of smiling, happy people.

The faces of the people at her meetings were grim, and smiled very little. But they were faces, nevertheless.

Also, Father, I knew so little. I had been shut away from the world for years. I quietly listened as they droned on, almost in a foreign language. There had been several more Big Bangs in other parts of the world that I didn't know anything about. The Clerics had built a giant wall separating Mexico and the US. Now they were building the same kind of wall on the northern border with Canada. It seemed like Muslims ruled most of the rest of the world, but the Clerics were determined that they were not going to take over here,

"Who gives a fuck about the Muslims. We got our own fucking Muslims. What's the difference? We need to blow those walls up. They're made this into a big prison camp!" Lucy said passionately at one meeting.

The people in the room all started shouting and stamping their feet in unison. "Blow the mother up! Blow the mother up! Blow the mother up!"

Father, my head was spinning! No wonder I had tuned out. What kind of weird world were these young people living in? I just couldn't follow their conversation. I didn't know what the hell they were talking about most of the time.

But I didn't tell Lucy that. But I guess she knew.

"Ok," she said, slowly shaking her head up and down. "Ok, Alexander. Now, do you have any advice?"

"Yeah. In fact, I do," I answered without hesitation. "First, you need to cool out that little asshole who calls himself a Colonel. Colonel my ass! That guy couldn't be a buck private where I come from! Imagine, wanting to kill innocent people. That's what started all of this bullshit in the first place."

As I spoke, I listened to myself, almost as if I was listening to a strange, yet vaguely familiar old voice. I hadn't heard that voice in years. It was strong, confident, boastful, full of fight.

Lucy also seemed surprised. She wasn't as quick to answer me back as she usually was.

"We have to fight back, Alexander," she said finally, "how else are we going to get those bastards off of us, with their fucking Bibles. I hate those goddamn Bibles! I hate those fucking Bibles!"

Lucy was practically foaming at the mouth. She was red-faced, mean-looking, her blue eyes bulging. I could see why her friends gave her a wide berth, and called her "commander." She was now a scary looking little bitch, that was for sure, Father!

Still, she also seemed young, petulant, and unreasonable.

I held up my hand to silence her. "You need the people on your side. The people have to rise up in support of you. Don't forget that. You can target caregivers, that's not a bad idea. But, what you need is what we had in the military: intelligence. You to need to watch carefully. Gather information. Know your targets. Be smarter than them. One mistake on your part and those preachers will turn everyone against you. A lot of folks are still fooled by them. You have to turn everyone against them. They know people are Scared. Scared of Cancer. Scared of another Big Bang. Scared of everything. That's the key to their power. You have to make people feel powerful again. If you scare them with random attacks, that's just going to make them even more scared, and that is just what the Clerics want."

Final Chapter

From that point on, Lucy turned to me, discussing with me in great details what she planned on doing. Sometimes she listened to me; sometimes she didn't. But she got what she wanted: my involvement. I became, in essence, Father, her Joint Chief of Staff, so to speak.

I was still living in Mother's apartment but was spending almost every night with Lucy. We both just did not want to be away from each other. Ever! And Anna K. Libid? Just months after Lucy and I had started our affair, she took ill. It was almost as if she had kept her good health long enough to know that Lucy would not be alone if she died.

But this also meant that I would soon be faced with decisions. What if something bad happened to Anna; then what should I do? Should I abandon Mother's apartment at long last and move in with Lucy? That made more sense, in that her place was larger, and in many ways, better than mine.

It sat facing the ocean. Her room, which we stayed most of the time, was large and sun-filled. This was so important because of the 35 watts light bulbs. It was also filled with large, expensive, comfortable Old World furniture.

"This was my father's room. It's just as he left it," she once explained to me. As she made her comment, I saw for the first time the Manhattan Syndrome. I could feel her sadness and sense of great loss.

The lit candles, after we turned the lamp out, gave her room an even more warm, embracing feeling. I could see the ocean and hear it on nights when it became fully alive. Then, the ocean also gave me much comfort—in many ways more than wine or sex or doo wop, mainly because I knew it had seen so much and will see even more, as the life that once crawled out of it to walk on solid ground, lives, dies and lives and dies—until it is all over, and then the mighty ocean once again reclaim everything. We are the water planet despite what we on land might think. That much is sure.

But, could I give up Mother's apartment? It would mean a breaking away not only from a comfortable space but a breaking away from Mother. Each day I spent in that place, I felt her presence. I saw her sitting on the couch, at the dinner table, cleaning up my room. Could I really fully throw myself in with this often-scary young person I barely knew?

***

I sat with Anna K. Libid, as Lucy left for one of her meetings.

"Look after grandmother. I don't think she's well. Please don't leave until I get back. Okay?" Lucy spoke in a low ominous whisper, as if Anna might overhear us, as she kissed me goodbye and gave me a hug at the door.

"Really. She getting worse?"

"Yes."

"Are you going to do anything about it. I mean, what can we do to help her?"

"I'm going to go see my caregiver in the morning. I hate that nosy bitch, but I need to know what to do in case something happens to grandmother. Look, Alexander. I've got to go. We'll talk about it when I get back. Love you. Love you."

With that, Lucy left me alone with Anna. I sat down across from her in the same seat I sat in when we first met months ago. I could see by the look on her face that she was not feeling well. The happy, jolly look was gone. Now, all of that fat just sagged. It seemed as if her entire body was melting into her fat body.

But, for some reason, Father, I wanted to talk to her, to hear her advice, to listen to her, as I once listen to Mother.

"I'm so glad Lucy found you, Alex. She used to bother me all the time, 'who's that black man. You say you know him. I want to meet him.' I'd say, 'leave the poor man alone. Can't you see he's full of hurt? If he wants to meet you, he would say something.' Just let him be, child. But, for some reason, she just wanted to meet you so badly. I was almost as if God was telling her that you needed saving, and she was your angel of mercy."

Anna spoke softly, with none of the high drama and playfulness that she used have in her voice. It was hard to believe that it was only a few months ago when she sat here and charmed the life back into me.

Now she spoke quietly, introspectively, in Russian, as if Lucy was in the next room and she wanted to keep this conversation private, just between she and me.

"God provides. God willed it," I answered back just as low, just as softly, just as introspectively, my Russian now haven't fully come back because of my conversations with her these last few months.

In many ways, the moments I shared with Anna K. Libid were much more intimate than anything I shared with Lucy. For some strange reason, Father, I also felt that Mother was in the room with us, watching over our conversation, listening to us as we poured out our Russian souls to each other. When I was with Mrs. Libid, I was back with Mother, just she and I, sitting around our dinner table, talking about God, theater, mother Russia, or just bad, lying neighbors.

"Yes, God is good to us, isn't he?"

"Yes, he is," I answered.

"You take good care of her, you hear. She's a good girl. A little wild. She's Irish. Irish people are wild, not like Russians. I told my son, 'Don't marry that crazy woman. Find a nice Russian girl in Brighton Beach.' But he wanted to live in Manhattan with Lucy's mother.

"Poor child. Poor little Lucy. I love her so much. Alex, I really do. I tried to give her everything I could. If she hadn't been staying with us…just a little visit with grandma and grandpa—but you know how young men are when they're in heat.

"Don't notice a thing. Manhattan! Manhattan! Everything was Manhattan. Broke his father's heart. Killed him. I know it killed him. My husband was also named Alexander. I never told you that, did I? Only he spelled it in the Russian way, like the great Pushkin did. He wanted to name Lawrence, Alexander, but I said one is enough for me.

"My poor husband. Such a nice man. He drank some, that's all. He just sat and died. Never said another word. Not one word. It was so sad. It was so crazy back then, Alexander. But her mother turned out all right. She's nice girl.

"Who knew, Alexander? If Lawrence had stayed in Brighton Beach like you…had listened to his father and mother…maybe…but, then we wouldn't have Lucy, would we? She's all I have. Be careful not to call her Irish. She feels guilty. She thinks that I think that her mother killed my son by talking him out of Brighton Beach. Sometimes I say the wrong things. I talk with feeling instead of my mind. What made me say something like that? I just used to get so sad. Don't say anything about her being Irish. She's Russian. God, I love her so much. I…"

Her voice trailed off again, this time coming to a complete stop. She gave me a quick, meaningful glance and looked away. It was almost as if she had been talking to herself. She sighed deeply, looking down, looking inward.

For the first time, Father, I saw clearly the Manhattan Syndrome in full force. Being the great actress she is, she had managed to conceal it from me all of those months. Now her acting had ceased, and suddenly, there it was.

The candlelight flickered up and down, occasionally highlighting her old, sad, tired face.

"You black people have soul," she said, still looking as if I was not even in the room, and she was having this private conversation with herself.

"God, do you people have soul! You know what I mean, Alexander. Pushkin had soul. That's what made him so great. That's why your dear mother named you after him. That's why he was the greatest Russia ever. You know what I mean, Alexander."

For some reason, Anna K. Libid was calling me Alexander for the first time. The way she pronounced my name in Russian made it sound so formal, so serious.

"Yes Anna, I know what you mean."

"Soul is close to God, Alexander."

Anna looked up from her inner self and stared at me with unblinking eyes. She lowered her eyes and fell silent. We just sat quietly after that, for the rest of the evening until Lucy returned, not saying anything, both of us locked in our private world.

For some reason I decided that night not to stay with Lucy but to return home. Lucy gave me a look of deep disappointment. I saw a flash of real fear and longing on her face.

"I'll be back early tomorrow," I said, reassuring her.

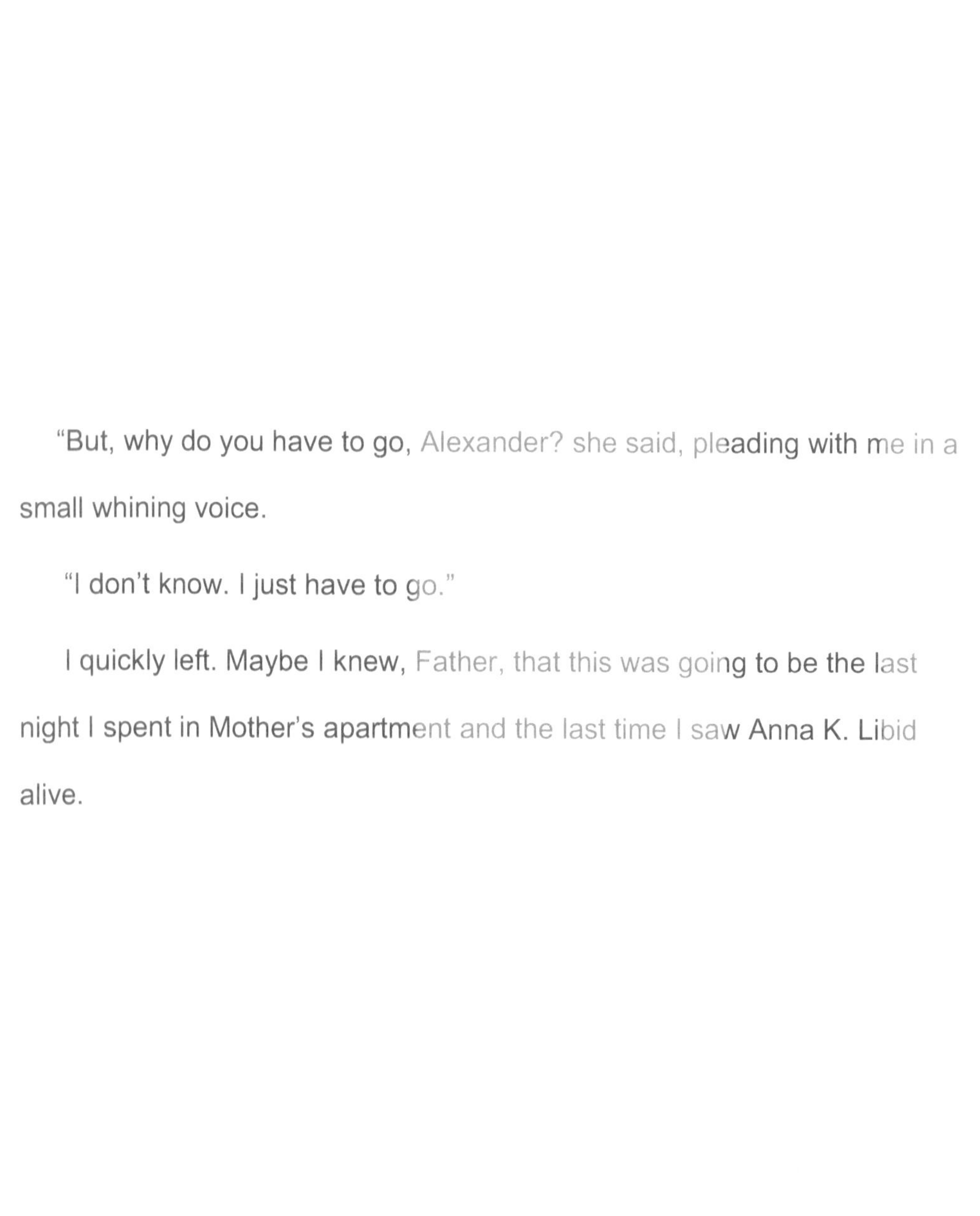

"But, why do you have to go, Alexander? she said, pleading with me in a small whining voice.

"I don't know. I just have to go."

I quickly left. Maybe I knew, Father, that this was going to be the last night I spent in Mother's apartment and the last time I saw Anna K. Libid alive.